BEAN THERE, DONE THAT

The Maggy Thorsen Mysteries from Sandra Balzo

UNCOMMON GROUNDS

GROUNDS FOR MURDER *

* *available from Severn House*

BEAN THERE, DONE THAT

A Maggy Thorsen Mystery

Sandra Balzo

This first world edition published 2008
in Great Britain and the USA by
SEVERN HOUSE PUBLISHERS LTD of
9–15 High Street, Sutton, Surrey, England, SM1 1DF.

British Library Cataloguing in Publication Data

Balzo, Sandra
  Bean there, done that. - (A Maggy Thorsen mystery)
  1. Thorsen, Maggie (Fictitious character) - Fiction
  2. Coffeehouses - Wisconsin - Milwaukee - Fiction
  3. Businesswomen - Wisconsin - Milwaukee - Fiction
  4. Murder - Wisconsin - Milwaukee - Fiction 5. Detective
  and mystery stories
  I. Title
  813.6[F]

  ISBN-13: 978-0-7278-6653-0   (cased)
  ISBN-13: 978-1-84751-073-0   (trade paper)

Typeset by Palimpsest Book Production Ltd.,
Grangemouth, Stirlingshire, Scotland.
Printed and bound in Great Britain by
MPG Books Ltd., Bodmin, Cornwall.

One

Here's a tip: if your ex-husband's mistress-cum-missus asks for your help in proving that he cheated on *her* while he was married to *you,* just say no.

And, whatever you do, don't invite her in for a cup of coffee.

'Wine?' I asked, stepping aside to let Rachel Slattery, now Rachel Slattery Thorsen, pass by.

Rachel frowned, wrinkling her pert little nose as she moved into my living room. 'It's a bit early for me, Maggy,' she said. 'But maybe . . . a mimosa?'

Of course. Let me just pop some champagne to celebrate her arrival. 'It was my morning to open the store,' I said. 'To me, noon is the new five o'clock.'

I don't know why I was bothering to explain. I'd started my coffeehouse, Uncommon Grounds, only because Ted, my former husband and Rachel's current one, dumped me for her. Ted being a dentist and Rachel his hygienist, they'd apparently fallen in love over the spit sink.

Anyway, my point is that when you got right down to it, it was Rachel's fault I had been upright and brewing coffee at five thirty a.m. 'It's wine or nothing.'

'A white Zin?'

The next best thing to nothing. 'Coming up!'

I left her with Frank, the sheepdog I inherited when my son Eric went off to college in Minnesota, and headed for the kitchen. Behind me, I heard Frank rouse himself and then, with a groan, settle back down on the hearth of the unlighted fireplace. At least one male in the family wasn't enamored of Rachel.

I poured the leavings of a bottle of red Zinfandel into a

glass for her and topped it off with flat 7-UP. Then I opened a fresh bottle of old vine Zin for myself.

When I went back in, Rachel was seated on the couch. She was wearing a short skirt and boots and, I had to admit, looked adorable. Lucky Ted: he'd managed to snag a younger woman just as the dress code he'd loved so much the first time around – minis, boots, platform shoes – cycled back into fashion.

'Thank you,' Rachel said, accepting the glass from me and sipping delicately. 'Ooooo, this is delicious.'

'I thought you'd like it.' I took a bracing belt of my real Zin. Then I sank into the chair across from her. 'Now, tell me again why you're here?'

'It's really quite simple.' She set down her glass. 'Ted told me that you save all your old calendars. Stack them up for years. I was hoping I could take a little peek.'

The subject of my calendars probably came up as Ted was telling her what an unrepentant pack-rat I was. I thought I was merely being prudent. Want to know when in 1996 we'd gone to the Bahamas? I could tell you. Not to mention, what year we put a new roof on the house, the day the refrigerator repairman came in 2004, or the exact date and time of our son Eric's high school graduation party. Which, coincidentally, was the day before Ted dropped the R-bomb.

'And you want these because . . .'

'I already told you.' Rachel rolled her eyes. 'You wrote down where Ted went for conferences and training.'

'That's true,' I admitted. 'Along with where he was staying and, before cellulars, a contact phone number.'

'I'm interested in more recent trips, say, the two years before he . . . uh, left you.'

For *her*.

'You mean the two years he was bopping you?' I asked pleasantly.

'Well, yes.' She tugged down her skirt and gave me a nervous smile.

'Don't you know where he was?' I asked. 'Weren't you with him on all those trips?'

Rachel leaned forward. 'That's what I thought,' she said in a low voice. 'But apparently not.'

'Hard as it might be for you to imagine, I suppose Ted could have gone to a legitimate dental conference or two without you.' Though looking at Little Miss Tooth De-Lay, with her short skirt and long legs, it was pretty hard for even me to imagine it.

'You don't keep trophies from dental conferences,' Rachel said, rifling through her patent leather YSL tote. YSL, as in Yves Saint Laurent. Rachel should know something about trophies. She was one.

'Excuse me?' I asked politely.

She came out with a stack of plastic rectangles. 'Trophies,' Rachel repeated, handing them to me.

'These are key cards.' I shuffled through them quickly. 'From hotels.'

'Exactly.'

I shrugged. 'So you want to turn him in for not returning his room key to the desk?'

'You just don't get it, do you?' Rachel leapt up dramatically. 'He's been cheating on me. Now *and* then.' She pointed to the keys and burst into tears.

I handed her a tissue. The woman managed to look good, even when she cried. It should have pissed me off, but under the circumstances, I was heartened. If Ted had cheated on someone who could even *cry* pretty, then maybe his cheating had more to do with him than it did with either Rachel *or* me.

Not that it mattered. I was now a self-confident entrepreneur with a coffeehouse of my own. What my ex thought or didn't think about me was neither here nor there.

Yet . . . it managed to hover everywhere. Old habits die hard.

'Rachel, a few hotel room keys don't prove—'

'My brother caught them in the act,' she choked out as she collapsed on to the couch sniffling. 'Not that I didn't suspect something was going on.'

I imagined Rachel would be pretty good at recognizing

the signs of an affair, given that she'd been on the other side of one.

With a sigh, Frank hefted himself off the floor, staggered over to her and collapsed with his head on her feet. Good ol' Frank, providing comfort wherever he lurched.

'I'm sorry Ted cheated on you,' I said, as Rachel leaned down to pat him. I was surprised to realize I genuinely meant it. 'But if you have that kind of proof –' I held up the key cards – 'what are these for?'

'I told you,' she said, 'they're trophies.'

'Soooo, you think he kept a key for every –' I searched for the right word – 'assignation?'

Rachel quirked her head.

'Bop session?' I tried.

'Oh, yes,' she said eagerly, 'and that's why I need the calendars.' She took the keys back from me. 'You know my family is in the hotel business.'

I nodded. The Slatterys were the Hiltons of southeastern Wisconsin, or so they fancied themselves. Rachel, Ted had told me when she first came to work for him, wanted nothing to do with the family business.

'Well, you may not know it,' Rachel was holding up a key card, 'but these contain information.'

'Isn't that an Internet myth?' I picked up my wine glass. 'You know, the old "don't leave your key because your charge card number is stored on it" scare?'

'It's true that personal information like your credit card number is not usually encrypted on them,' Rachel said. Suddenly she didn't sound like such a ditz. She sounded like a hotel heiress. 'But they do have the dates of your stay, the room number and a code that can be traced back to other stuff in the hotel computer.'

I was starting to understand why she wanted the calendars. 'So, you're saying that you could tell what dates he stayed where?'

'With the right equipment,' Rachel said. 'And my brother has the right equipment.'

I'd heard that a lot of the area's young females agreed with that.

Rachel continued. 'I want to check the key cards against where Ted *said* he was, according to your calendars, and cross-reference that with times I know *I* wasn't with him.'

'So you're trying to catch him in a lie,' I said. 'But a lie to *me*? Why?'

'Because then I can prove that he had no intention of being faithful. Which I'm hoping will put him in breach of the prenup he signed.'

'Your prenup says he can cheat after you were married, but not before?'

The roll of the eyes again. 'Of course not. But my lawyer says that if Ted entered into the prenup fraudulently, we might be able to throw out even the small stipend he'd receive.'

My first thought was: Ted, Ted, Ted – what have you gotten yourself into? My second was: how could this affect Eric and me?

After a few seconds, Rachel started to squirm. 'So, say something.'

'I'm just trying to get my arms around this,' I said. 'You want my help in nailing Ted for his nailing someone else, when he was already nailing you, while he was married to me.'

'Exactly.'

'But why should I do that? I have a son to think of. If Ted goes belly-up financially, he won't be able to pay for Eric's education.'

A sigh. 'That's pretty selfish of you, Maggy.' She stomped her fashionably shod little foot. Dislodged, Frank turned tail and ran. 'Ted sinned, damn it!'

I squinted at her. 'Umm, you do understand that when you were "seeing" Ted, *both* of you were sinning, technic-ally.'

Rachel cocked her head.

'The seventh commandment,' I tried. '"Thou shalt not commit adultery"?'

Rachel gasped. 'It wasn't adultery, Maggy. We were in love.'

Her blue eyes clouded over as she seemed to remember

her reason for darkening both my doorway and my day. '*Were*,' she repeated, sniffling.

I pulled a Kleenex out of the emergency box I kept on the end table.

'Besides,' Rachel said, taking the tissue, 'that was before I found God.' She blew her nose loudly.

Ted had never been much of a churchgoer, but maybe Rachel sought out counseling when things had started to go sour. 'So are you attending Christ Christian?' CC was the big church just down Poplar Creek Road from me. 'Pastor Shepherd is a good guy.'

Langdon Shepherd was Christ Christian's minister. And, yes, people flocked there.

Except for Rachel apparently.

'Not yet. But I absolutely plan on working my way up to going to church,' Rachel said devoutly. 'I had an awakening – a revelation, really – on my way to Schultz's Market after Stephen told me about seeing Ted and his slut.'

So she went to the market after finding out about her whore-hound of a husband. Maybe Rachel was shopping for something to console herself. You know, like cookie-dough ice cream. Or a knife.

But back to me. 'Let me get this straight. You're saying that you are absolved for screwing my husband because you hadn't stumbled over God on the way to the grocery store yet?'

'Ted always said you were too flip, Maggy. You should stop it.' Rachel glanced apprehensively up at the ceiling of my living room like she expected divine retribution to come crashing through it. '*He* doesn't like it.'

I wasn't sure if she was talking about God or Ted. Though at one time, they had been pretty much synonymous in Rachel's book.

She sniffed again. 'I was betrayed by Ted. Led astray, like a lamb to the frying pan.' A shadow of confusion crossed her face. 'Or is it into the fire?'

'To the slaughter,' I supplied.

'Ugh,' she said, scrunching her nose. 'That's even worse.

But the point is, Maggy, that I didn't know I was sinning. The Bible says "ignorance is bliss".'

Not unless the poet Thomas Gray was an apostle. 'That isn't from . . .' Recognizing my folly, I stopped.

'And the Bible also says "to err is human, to forgive divine."' Rachel wagged a finger my way. 'You should remember that, Maggy.'

Me? I was too busy trying to remember which poet was responsible for Rachel's second quote. Donne, Milton? No, no, Alexander Pope, that was it. Who said my English Lit class would never come in handy?

'I'm not feeling very divine today,' I muttered. And if I was going to 'err', it was going to be on the side of caution. I mean, how did I know if Rachel was telling me the truth? Maybe she wanted my calendars for some other reason. Maybe something that Ted had put her up to, something more sinister. Something that had to do with *me*.

OK, so I had trust issues – a residual effect of Ted's affair that no one warned me about. I just couldn't stop wondering what other things he – and pretty much everyone else around me – might be hiding.

Rachel was looking at me like a kitten whose ball of yarn had just disappeared under the couch. Bewildered by the yarn's audacity, but certain something could be worked out. 'You can't still be holding a grudge.'

Still? The divorce was less than a year old. Admittedly a lifetime to a mere kid of twenty-five.

'Then *you've* already forgiven the bimbo Ted is bonking?' I asked her dryly.

Rachel's eyes narrowed. 'Are you being factious, Maggy? Ted says you have a nasty habit of that.'

Jesus, did these people have nothing better to do than talk about me? And study the 'Word a Day' calendar? 'I think you mean facetious,' I said.

Not that I was above creating a little internal conflict, too.

'Anyway, you have the keys and I have the calendars,' I said. 'I doubt that you're willing to turn over the key cards to me and I have no intention of handing my personal calendars over to you. Seems like we have a stalemate.'

'He's been too busy to get stale,' Rachel sniffed.

I laughed, surprised at her quickness. My response elicited a tiny grin from Rachel. 'How about this?' she said. 'You find the calendars and we go see my brother together.'

I glanced at the clock on the mantle of the fireplace that took up one entire wall of my living room. My robin's-egg blue stucco living room. I'd planned to paint the room post-haste when I'd moved into my tiny post-divorce house, but now I barely noticed the color. As my grandmother said, 'You can get used to hanging if you hang long enough.'

'Come on, Maggy,' Rachel was saying, 'aren't you even the tiniest bit curious?'

Curious? Of course I was curious. I wasn't an idiot, after all. I'd entertained the possibility that Rachel hadn't been the first. At the time of my divorce, though, I hadn't wanted to know. It was bad enough acknowledging that the last two years of my marriage had been a sham. I couldn't face the possibility there had been more women, going even further back. That we'd *never* had what I'd imagined we did.

'Don't ask questions you don't want answers to,' I muttered to myself.

Rachel didn't say anything. I glanced over and saw that she was waiting. No expression. No tears. No begging. No reasoning. Just waiting for me to do what she knew, somehow, I would do.

Now *I* felt like the kid. I sighed. 'Are you sure *you* want the answers?'

My ex-husband's trophy wife met my gaze. 'Not knowing doesn't change what happened, Maggy. It doesn't make it go away. It only makes you . . . stupid.'

From the mouths of babes. Or babe, in this case.

This woman was sharper – and gutsier – than she appeared.

Two

I needed to drop some magazines by Uncommon Grounds, so Rachel and I arranged to meet at the Slattery Arms at two thirty.

She pulled out of my driveway first, leading the way down Poplar Creek Drive in her Cadillac Escalade, while I followed in my brand new Ford Escape. I had the windows down and the radio was blasting 'Hot Fun in the Summertime'. The old Sly & the Family Stone song was resurrected by the local radio stations anytime an unseasonably warm day popped up. In this case, our warm day – approaching sixty-five degrees Fahrenheit – was in mid-April.

Like 'Hot Fun', the old saw, 'If you don't like the weather, wait five minutes,' also was being repeated ad nauseam on radio, television and in every street-corner conversation. Meteorologists love Milwaukee. Epic electrical storms, vicious tornadoes, torturous heat, freezing cold, snow up the wazoo. We had it all. Sometimes in the same day.

I stepped on the brake to allow some distance between me and Rachel. The woman drove her Escalade like a nineteen-foot, six thousand-pound bumper car. I continued to stay well back as we turned right on to Brookhill Road, afraid that if she stopped too fast, my little Escape and I would find ourselves crammed up the rear of her monster truck, lost forever among the fourteen-way bucket seats and heated cup holders.

As I turned right again into the parking lot of Benson Plaza, Rachel tooted her horn and continued on Brookhill Road toward downtown Milwaukee. We'd located Uncommon Grounds in Benson Plaza so commuters could zip in to pick up their morning coffee on the way to work. The plaza was L-shaped, with Uncommon Grounds on the short leg of the L, facing Brookhill Road. On the longer side of the L, where Goddard's Pharmacy and a grocery store were located, business probably was hopping with weekend shoppers. Our side, though, was quieter on Saturdays.

In fact, when I pulled into the lot there wasn't a single car there. Before Tony Bruno had retired and sold the dental practice next door, he'd had regular Saturday hours. The new owners opened only every other Saturday afternoon for a free dental clinic, leaving the place dead most of the time on the weekend. Maybe Caron and I should rethink our weekend hours.

Caron Egan was my friend and partner in Uncommon Grounds. She and our new barista, Amy, must have parked in the back lot – the innards of the L. I, on the other hand, regularly parked as close to the front door as possible. It drove Caron crazy. She believed we should leave the closest spots for customers.

I took a more marketing-oriented point of view. When the store was empty – today being a case in point – our cars made it look like we had customers. When we were busy, I figured people could walk. It was a whole lot cheaper than an athletic trainer at sixty dollars an hour.

As I got out of the car with the stack of coffee trade magazines Caron had been harping at me to bring back, a woman came around the corner and paused in front of Uncommon Grounds.

'We're open,' I called to her. 'It's just a little quiet this afternoon. The nice weather and all.'

The woman wore a parka with the hood up and didn't seem all that impressed by the balmy temperatures. Probably a snowbird back from Florida and not yet accustomed to the cooler climate. Each year they returned to their homes in flocks and fired up their furnaces for a month longer than those of us who had weathered a Wisconsin winter.

Me, I remembered the May blizzard that dropped eight inches of snow on southeastern Wisconsin well enough to be grateful for any day above freezing, regardless of season. I also didn't put the shovel away until the Fourth of July. In other words, I was a native Wisconsinite.

The woman just waved her fingers vaguely at me and continued past the shop to the dental clinic next door.

'Stop in for coffee,' I called after her. 'Make that teeth-cleaning worthwhile.'

She turned and gave me a self-conscious half-smile. She was younger than I'd thought, probably in her twenties, and missing a front tooth.

'Oh, sorry,' I said. 'Accident?'

She nodded shyly and the hood of her jacket started to fall back. She righted it and moved on.

As she did, the sleigh bells on the door of Uncommon Grounds jangled and Caron stuck her head out. 'Are you chasing away customers again?'

'Nah, just dental patients.'

'The woman in the mauve puffy jacket who just came past?' Amy asked from behind the counter. 'She should have come in for coffee, the poor thing. She always looks like she's freezing. I think she's one of the clinic's low-income patients. She's been here the last couple of Free Saturdays.'

'How ever do people get here from the city?' Caron asked, letting me pass by before closing the door. 'It's nearly two miles to the nearest bus.'

'There *are* people here in the suburbs who can't afford a dentist,' I pointed out. Me, for one, now that my free ticket – marriage to Ted – had been punched.

'That's right,' Amy said. 'I read an article that said it's a misconception that poverty is only in the cities. There are just as many poor people in the suburbs. We just don't see them.'

Caron flushed. 'I didn't mean anything by it. It's just . . .' There was an uncomfortable pause as she trailed off.

'Whatcha doing?' I asked to break the tension.

'Inventory,' Caron said, going back to the shelves.

I followed. 'I have your issues of *Coffee and Me*,' I said, proffering the magazines.

She looked at the dates on them. 'We've gotten two more since these.'

'So why have you been nagging me to bring them back?'

'Because I keep back issues.' She had returned to the acrylic bin she was emptying. 'Besides, it's good training for you. You should return what you borrow.'

'Thanks, Mom,' I said, hoping Rachel didn't plan to return what *she* had borrowed.

Caron didn't respond. She was surrounded by ten-pound bags of coffee and was making notations on a clipboard.

'Still a bean-counter, huh?' I tried again.

Caron and I had worked together years ago at First National Bank, though neither of us had been on the money side of the business. I did public relations and event management and Caron had been an ad copywriter.

I'd gotten Caron, her husband Bernie and the minivan in our divorce settlement. Ted had kept his family's fishing cabin in Lake Verde and the rest of our friends. Not much of a loss, because they'd all been his to begin with.

Caron gave the bean-counter joke the laugh it deserved.

'That's not funny.' She held out a scoop of coffee beans. 'Does this look like Breakfast Blend or Sunrise to you? I think the bins may be switched.'

'Sunrise,' I guessed, figuring I had a fifty-fifty shot at being right.

Caron gave it a sniff. 'You sure?'

Before I could answer, Amy chimed in. Literally.

'Maggy's right,' she said, nodding her head. 'Sunrise is umber-colored, where Breakfast Blend is tawnier, remember?'

I didn't know umber from tawny any more than I did Breakfast Blend from Sunrise. I had a more pressing question for Amy now that she had stepped out from behind the counter. 'Is that a wind chime on your ear?'

'Don't you love it?' Amy flicked the dangling earring with her finger and it rang out like an actual wind chime. Only smaller.

She cocked her ear to hear . . . her ear. 'Pentatonic scale. Minor, I think, don't you?'

'I do,' I said solemnly. Amy had the most eclectic base of

knowledge I'd ever been exposed to. If she had said her earring played 'Amazing Grace', I would have agreed with her.

'It plays "Amazing Grace",' she said.

I looked at her.

'Really.' She removed the tiny chime. '"Amazing Grace" uses the pentatonic scale. Just the black keys on the piano.'

She dangled the earring delicately between her thumb and forefinger. 'If you find me a toothpick, I'll show you.'

Personally, I would have paid money to see Amy perform 'Amazing Grace' on her earring using a toothpick. Unfortunately, Caron didn't agree.

'We have to finish this inventory.' She dropped the lid on the bean bin. 'Besides, we don't have any toothpicks.'

I wasn't sure that was true. Being a faithful partner, though, I went along. 'Caron's probably right. Would a chopstick work? I think I have the ones from Chinese take-out yesterday.'

Caron shot me a dirty look.

But Amy was shaking her head, even as she deftly replaced the earring. She had lots of practice with piercings. Six in her left ear, three in her right, two in her . . .

'Where are your lip rings?' I asked.

She wrinkled her nose. 'I thought it was too much, with the wind chime and all.'

'Good point,' I said, ignoring Caron who was still staring daggers at me for perpetuating the conversation. She'd been the one who *had* to have Amy in the first place. Now that the rock star of Brookhill's baristas worked for us, though, Caron seemed impatient with her rock star*ness*.

To be honest, Caron seemed impatient a lot these days. I wondered if things were OK at home.

I didn't have time to inquire because the chimes – this time the ones on the door – jangled. The newcomer was Sarah Kingston, Brookhills' real estate agent extraordinaire and what passed for my closest friend.

As she came in, Sarah was whistling, 'Oh, What a Beautiful Mornin''. Believe me when I tell you this was out of character for her.

'You're in an awfully chipper mood,' I said suspiciously.

Sarah finished out the song before she answered. Right about the time the cattle were 'standing like statues', Caron snagged a bag of trash and slammed out the back door, with a muttered, 'It's not even morning, for God's sake.'

'What's her problem?' Sarah asked, petering out on the chorus.

I shrugged. 'Don't know, but she's been irritable for about a week now.'

'Since her birthday last week,' Amy contributed from where she was tallying numbers.

Uh-oh. 'I forgot about her birthday,' I admitted. 'Is she mad?'

'I don't think so,' Amy said. 'I think *she* wants to forget her birthday.'

Caron was a month older than me, which put her at forty-five.

'That's ridiculous.' Sarah was shaking her head. 'Forty-five is the new twenty. Look at me.' She spread her arms out wide so her baggy jacket flapped open like wings above her equally baggy trousers. 'I've quit smoking and started exercising. Cardio and stomach crunches. I've never felt better in my life.'

Why is it that when a person – say me, for example – falls off the fitness bandwagon, it seems like the rest of the world – even someone who once mistook a muscle for a tumor – hops on?

'You do look fabulous,' Amy said. 'How much weight have you lost?'

'Fourteen.' Sarah was studying Amy's face. 'Why are you wearing just one wind chime?'

'I thought asymmetrical was the way to go. What do you think?' Amy said, turning her head back and forth, jingling to and fro.

Sarah pursed her lips. 'You're right,' she said after a moment. 'Two would have been ordinary. By wearing one, you've taken it to the next level.'

First Sarah was exercising, now she was giving accessorizing tips. I didn't know if I should be happy for my friend or afraid of her.

'Are you sure you're still Sarah? Or has someone else taken over your body?'

'As long as they give it back in better shape than they took it, I'm OK with that.' Sarah pulled out her cellphone to check the time.

The action reminded me of Rachel, which in turn reminded me of Ted, which depressed me.

'Listen,' Sarah was saying, 'I have to run.' She giggled. Sarah never giggles. 'Not literally, of course. I run at five.'

I just looked at her.

'In the morning.'

That's it. I was going to start exercising tomorrow. And I was never going to eat again. Ever.

Sarah was still talking. It would probably take a stake through her heart to stop her. 'I need to make a couple more stops and then get home and change. I'm meeting someone for an early dinner downtown and the sunset walking tour of historic buildings.'

'Walking tour?' I asked before I could help myself. Now Sarah was walking? And touring something other than a home she had listed? What was next?

'Sure.' Sarah dug through her voluminous bag and pulled out a flyer. 'My friend leads the tour for the Visit Milwaukee Center. She said she thought I'd enjoy it, being in real estate myself.'

This was what was next. Sarah had friends. I mean, besides me.

She handed me the brochure. 'A lot of the buildings in Milwaukee are changing hands or being turned into condos. The tour, I guess, gives you the inside scoop. The skele-tons in the architectural closet, so to speak.'

She slung her bag on to her shoulder. 'Well, mustn't be late. Ta-ta.'

A jangle of the bells and she was gone.

'*Ta-ta?*' Amy and I asked in unison.

When Caron came back, she wasn't in a better mood.

'Somebody left the gate unlocked again,' she complained as she put a new plastic liner in the waste can.

'Guess it's a good thing there's nothing to steal in the dumpsters.' I was trying to be positive.

Caron shook her head impatiently. 'It's not what they take, Maggy. It's what they leave.'

As she spoke, she picked up the flyer I'd put on the counter and fanned herself. I didn't know if it was the un-seasonably warm weather that was bothering her or a hot flash. I thought it best not to ask.

'C'mon, Caron, lighten up. It's trash, not bodies or toxic waste. Are you OK?'

She ignored my question. 'There are two computer screens and what looks like a brand new box spring out there. Oh, and some draperies. We could furnish a house. The trash guys come on Friday. Computers and furniture aren't allowed.' She looked like she was going to cry.

I patted her on the shoulder. 'I know, I know. My brother still has a Commodore 64 he doesn't know what to do with.'

Caron sniffed and cracked a smile. 'A museum, perhaps?'

I grinned back, happy to make at least a little headway with her. I knew I wasn't always as concerned about these types of things as Caron was. I'd like to say it was because I had a life. I didn't. I just didn't give a damn.

'Tell you what?' I offered. 'I'll investigate the dumpster situation and see who's leaving it unlocked.'

'And the mattress and all?' Caron asked hopefully.

'Once we make sure the other tenants are locking the gate, we won't have to worry about people dumping things in the dumpsters besides us. As for what's already there, I'll try to sweet-talk the trash guys into taking that on Friday. If they won't, we'll just pay extra and be done with it.' I put my hand on Caron's shoulder. 'Make sense?'

She nodded her head.

I studied her face. 'And I ask again: are you OK?'

'Sure.' She slid the trash basket back under the counter and straightened up. 'I'm just old and cranky.'

'You are not,' I assured her. 'You're young and cranky.'

'Shuddup.' She smacked away my hand. 'You'll get yours in a month, when you're as old as me.'

'Actually, I'm hoping to get mine tonight,' I said with a grin. 'Pavlik's coming over.'

The subject of Brookhills County Sheriff Jake Pavlik immediately improved Caron's mood, as I hoped it would. Long-married, she enjoyed living vicariously through my new single status. Why, I had no idea. I was certain she and Bernie were having way more sex than Pavlik and me.

Caron was smiling and chatting with Amy when I left. I was a bit more chipper myself, no longer fixated on Rachel's visit this morning. That mood lasted until I got out into the parking lot and saw Ted.

My ex.

Rachel's husband.

Rachel's perhaps future ex.

Liar.

Cheater.

Father of my son.

'Afternoon,' I said as pleasantly as I could manage. Ted was in running clothes and sweating profusely, thank God. That meant hugging was out of the question, so we'd be spared one of the awkward hug-or-don't-hug moments that an 'amicable' divorce engenders.

'I'm disgusting,' he said, holding up his hands.

'I know.' I'm sure my smile was bigger than he expected.

'Good to see you, though.' He was looking at me suspiciously. 'How've you been?'

'Perfect. Out running, I see.' It was a safe subject. Fitness freaks are always happy to chat about their workouts. It would give me the requisite five minutes of polite conversation I felt we should engage in as modern ex-spouses. Then I was out of there and heading toward a date with a man who appreciated me. And would, I hoped, someday have sex with me.

'I'm training for a marathon,' Ted said cheerfully. 'Is Sarah here? I said I'd run with her tomorrow, but I have to cancel.'

'Sarah's running a marathon, too?' Great. Now *I'd* have to run a marathon. Not to mention that my best friend was hanging out with my ex.

'Nah.' Ted had his hands over his head, stretching.

His short jacket moved up and I could see abs. Not just stomach, you understand, *abs*. A six-pack. The last time I'd seen a six-pack on Ted's stomach, he'd been drinking from it.

I took a good look at my ex-husband. He'd always been handsome. Six-feet tall, sandy brown hair, green eyes. I'd fallen for him the first time we'd talked. He had a way of looking at you, really looking at you, as he spoke. It made you think you were the center of his universe for that moment. It had made me want to be the center of his universe forever. And to make him the same of mine.

'Forever' had lasted nearly twenty years. Or eighteen if you subtracted the Rachel Years. Longer than for most couples, I guessed. Question was, how many more of those eighteen were . . .

'. . . so sometimes Sarah comes running with Emma and me,' Ted finished.

Emma? 'I'm sorry,' I said, 'but I was thinking about something else. Who did you say Emma was?'

Ted rolled his eyes. He and Rachel must have a blast rolling their respective eyeballs at each other. 'Emma Byrne. She and I went to dental school together. She was over to the house a bunch of times, with her boyfriend. Griffin something or other. You remember.'

I did now. Emma had been born in Ireland and, where I thought of people of Irish descent as having brown or red hair and green eyes, her hair was raven black, her eyes a startling navy blue. She was memorable and I thought I'd seen that memory walking through the parking lot of Benson Plaza last week.

'You know, I think she's part of the dental group that bought the practice next door.'

'She is,' Ted confirmed. 'She's also Sarah's dentist. Emma has been on her for years to quit smoking. Nasty habit, smoking. Yellows your teeth, causes gum problems.'

Not to mention those lesser problems of cancer and heart disease. I tried not to wonder about how closely Ted and Emma Byrne had stayed 'in touch' over the years.

'Once Sarah gave up the cigarettes,' Ted said, 'Emma thought running might give her a reason to stay off them.'

Talk about your full-service dentist. 'So how do you fit into this health kick?' I asked.

Another roll of the eyes. 'I *told* you. Emma and I are training for the Milwaukee Marathon.'

'But not Sarah.' I just wanted to be sure hell hadn't frozen over.

'Not yet, but I have to give her credit. She's running about four miles with us before she drops off at the Donut Hole.'

'Now there's the Sarah I know and love,' I said, smiling. 'Except for the four miles part.'

'People change.' Ted said it quietly.

The switch in mood startled me. If he wanted to debate the point, I might argue that it wasn't so much people who changed, but what we knew about them. Had Ted loved me and then changed his mind, or had he never really loved me at all and I'd just become aware of it?

'What about Rachel?' I asked abruptly.

'What about Rachel?' Ted asked back, seeming surprised.

'Is she running, too?' It was a lame though fair question. When Rachel had worked for Ted, they used to 'run' together every lunchtime. Like little fornicating Energizer bunnies.

'She trained for awhile, but she had to quit. She's . . . busy.' His tone was evasive.

'Really?' I said, not able to stop myself. 'To hear her tell it, you're the one who's been busy.'

'Me?' Ted looked confused. Then he looked worried. 'When did you talk to Rachel?'

I shrugged. 'Just ran into her. Listen, I have to go.'

Then I shut my mouth and left. Too bad it was thirty seconds too late.

Three

Rachel and I had agreed to meet in the lobby of the Slattery Arms. The Arms was the flagship of the hotel chain and the management and sales offices were housed there.

'We're going to have to make this quick,' Rachel said as she pressed the up button by the elevators. 'I have to look at a property later this afternoon.'

'Are you moving?'

'Me? No way. Once I have it out with Ted, I plan to send *him* packing.'

'Ted doesn't have any idea that you—'

'Of course not.' An elevator arrived and we stepped in. Rachel pressed '8' and the doors slid closed. 'I want to wait until I have all the facts. Whatever gave you the idea I was moving?'

'You said you needed to look at a property this afternoon,' I reminded her.

'Oh, that.' She was checking her cellphone. 'We're considering buying the Hamilton and turning it into a Slattery.'

I was impressed. The Hamilton is a legendary old hotel – complete with obligatory ghost – about six blocks from Lake Michigan. Perfectly positioned downtown, it had gorgeous city and river views to the west and lake views to the east. The owners closed it down last year for renovations, but when building costs skyrocketed, they'd been caught short. I'd heard the Hamilton was going to be turned into condos, but apparently the Slattery family had other ideas.

'I didn't realize you were still involved with the family business,' I said to Rachel as we stepped off the elevator and on to the burgundy-carpeted foyer of the Slattery Hotels' business office.

'I wasn't, for a long time. I didn't want anything to do with the hotels.' She shrugged. 'But circumstances have changed. I need to step up.'

Maybe it was because we were on her turf or maybe it was because Rachel had inadvertently given me a glance of the shrewd woman beneath the miniskirt, but all vestiges of the ditz seemed to have disappeared.

In her place stood a hotel mogul. Or mogulette.

Rachel tapped on the ornate wooden door in front of us, but didn't wait for an answer before swinging it open.

The front door at Uncommon Grounds tinkles. My door at home, on the other hand, crunches – the result of Frank gnawing off the doorstop, leaving the plaster wall to be repeatedly pounded by the doorknob. The door of the Slattery offices did not tinkle, nor crunch. And creaking would have been unimaginable. The Slattery Arms door glided. A measured, dignified glide.

The man at the desk beyond that door wasn't so dignified. He was what Amy would call hot. Hell, *I'd* call him hot.

Stephen Slattery was shuffling through some papers on the receptionist's desk, sleeves of his white dress shirt rolled up, knot of his tie pulled down, blond hair rumpled. He grinned when he saw Rachel and came around the desk to hug her. 'Hey, you. How's everything?'

The words were conversational, but his tone implied more. I wasn't sure what Rachel had told her brother about why we were there, so I planned to keep my mouth shut and listen. Neither are things I do well.

Rachel, who was nearly a foot shorter than Stephen, grinned up at him. 'Just fine, Stevie. I told you not to worry about me.'

Stephen's gaze flickered over to me. His eyes were the color of dark chocolate. Seventy to eighty percent cocoa content. I know my chocolate.

'Stephen,' Rachel was saying, 'this is Maggy Thorsen. I don't think you've ever met.'

Since I'd skipped Rachel and Ted's nuptials, I was fairly certain that was true.

Stephen's eyebrows had shot up. 'I don't think so.' He stuck out his hand. 'Good to meet you, Mrs . . . umm, Ms . . .'

'I don't think "how to address your sister's husband's ex-wife" is covered in the etiquette books,' I said, taking his hand. 'Why don't you just call me Maggy?'

'Maggy – thank you,' Stephen said gratefully and we shook hands.

'Hello?' Rachel said.

I turned, thinking it was the kind of 'hello' loosely translated as 'are you aware of the fact you're an idiot?'. But Rachel was answering her cellphone.

'I didn't hear it ring, did you?' Stephen asked.

I shook my head. 'According to my son, there are ring-tones available that are high enough that most people can't hear them.'

'Like dog whistles?'

'Exactly,' I said, perhaps a little too readily. Afraid he might think I was calling his sister a dog, I backtracked. 'Well, not exactly. The younger a person is, the higher the registers they can hear. My son Eric can hear sounds I can't and since Rachel is closer to his age than . . .'

I slapped my mouth closed before I said, 'Ted's.'

Did I keep it closed, though?

Nah. What fun would that be?

'As we get older,' I babbled on, 'the higher ranges are the first thing to go. Which could explain why you, or we, didn't hear the ring.'

Those eyebrows rode up again. One of them had a little slice through it, like Stephen had fallen and cut himself as a kid.

'Not that I'm saying you're old,' I added hastily. 'I mean you're younger than me – much younger, I'm sure. Probably just lost that higher level at some rock concert.'

'The Grateful Dead,' he dead-panned.

I laughed. 'Right. More like the Smashing Pumpkins.'

'No, seriously.' He settled on to the edge of the desk. 'It was a Grateful Dead concert in 1985. I was fourteen or fifteen.' He touched his eyebrow. 'That's where this happened, too.'

'How?' I asked, while trying to do mental arithmetic. If Stephen was fifteen in 1985, that meant he wasn't as young as I'd assumed. All that tousled hair had made me miss the fine lines starting to show around the cocoa-colored eyes.

'A friend and I managed to worm our way up to the front row,' he said. 'The advantage of being a skinny kid, I thought. Little did I know that once you're up there, it's only you between the snow fence and ten thousand screaming, pushing people behind you.'

I gasped. 'Were you trampled?'

'No.' He rubbed the eyebrow. 'But I did manage to get the fence pole stuck in my eye – or close to my eye. I came home with blood streaming down my face. I thought my mother was going to kill me.'

Rachel snapped closed her phone. 'Which time?'

'The Grateful Dead concert.'

'Oh, that.' Rachel waved it away as inconsequential. 'Why ever were you talking about that?'

I looked at Stephen blankly. Stephen looked at me, equally blankly.

'Oh, wait,' I said, trying to track it back. 'We were talking about losing the higher registers of our hearing at rock concerts.'

'And again, I ask why?' She had dug a pen out of her tote and was making a note on the back of a crumpled receipt. Her tone seemed to insinuate that if we weren't talking about her, we should be sitting quietly with our hands folded.

'Because I didn't hear your phone ring,' Stephen explained.

Rachel rolled her eyes. 'It wasn't your ears. I have it on vibrate.'

The simplest explanation is usually the best. Not that I hadn't enjoyed the silly little tangent Stephen and I had taken off on.

'We were just exploring other alternatives,' he said, tossing me a grin.

'Right,' Rachel said. 'That's what you told Mother and Daddy every time you changed majors.'

She stuffed the note and the pen into her bag and checked her cellphone again. 'It's nearly three. We have to get moving here. I'm meeting a building inspector at the Hamilton in thirty minutes and God knows where I'll find parking around there with all the construction.' She held out her hand imperiously. 'The calendars, Maggy?'

I obediently dug the stack out of the bag I'd brought them in. In contrast to Rachel's designer tote, mine was brown and made of paper. With the aroma of onions still clinging to it. Can't say I'm not a hard act to follow.

I held the calendars out. Stephen didn't reach for them. 'Do you, umm ... I mean ...' He was turning red under the tan. Seemingly at a loss, he turned to Rachel. 'I mean, does she ...?'

'She knows,' Rachel said flatly.

Stephen turned sympathetically to me. 'I know this is tough on Rachel, but it can't be easy on you, either.'

I shrugged, trying for an air of sophisticated nonchalance. The grocery bag at my side and the yellowing papers in my hand weren't helping much.

Before I could actually say anything, Rachel spoke up. 'Personally, I'm surprised at how well Maggy is taking it.' She took the stack of mismatched calendars from me. 'I mean, he only cheated on me for a couple of years and I'm ready to kill the bastard. He cheated on her for what?' She looked over at me. 'Maybe a decade? Two?'

I wasn't sure which Rachel I liked more. Or less. The sweet ditz who was master of the malapropism or the hard-edged businesswoman who could do math.

'Two,' I said automatically. 'We were married nearly twenty.' In fact, Ted told me he was leaving me just two days shy of our twentieth anniversary. Must have been saving himself the cost of the anniversary card and dime-store bouquet.

'But I don't think he ...' I stopped. What did I really know, after all?

'Men are scum,' Rachel said flatly, moving to the desk

to sort through the calendars. Most of them were pocket-size, from my years at the bank. A few, though, had hung on the side of the refrigerator. As Rachel shuffled through the pile, I caught the occasional glimpse of Eric's artwork.

An involuntarily sniffle escaped. From me.

Stephen put his hand on the pile Rachel was rifling. She looked up at him in surprise and he tapped his watch.

'You said you needed to get to the Hamilton,' he reminded her. 'If the inspector finds rot, we'll have to rethink this deal.'

Rachel wrinkled her nose. 'Why would anyone build a hotel on wood pilings stuck in a swamp?'

I didn't have an answer to that.

'It was state-of-the-art in 1914,' Stephen explained. 'And it's not a swamp. There are underground water deposits between the river and the lake. If the pilings have been properly maintained, there should be no problem. In fact, the structure may be sounder than some more modern buildings.'

Rachel had pulled out her cellphone to confirm the time. 'Damn. I guess I should go.' She bit her lip. 'Do you suppose you can do this if I leave everything with you?'

'I have a meeting myself,' he said. 'But I can, after that. What years do you want me to check?' He looked from his sister to me and back.

Rachel already was getting out her car keys. 'Well, let's see. I started in the dental office three years ago, but we controlled ourselves for at least two months.'

Good of them.

Rachel was looking all dreamy-eyed, like she'd forgotten how the sandman had bitten her in the butt. 'The attraction was there from the moment we met,' she said. 'We both felt it, we said so after we made love that first time.'

Stephen cleared his throat to get her attention, cocking his head toward me.

'I'm still in the room,' I confirmed with a little wave.

Rachel rolled her eyes. 'I know that. I just wanted you to know that I'm not a complete slut. Ted and I were in love.'

I didn't say anything. I knew I didn't have to. Like I said, Rachel wasn't dumb.

Sure enough, her blue eyes welled up. 'Or I thought we were,' she whispered.

'Listen,' Stephen said, putting his arm around her and walking her toward the door. 'You go and I'll sort through Maggy's calendars and see if I can match them to the room keys.'

'Oopsy, that means you'll need them.' Rachel dug through her tote again to come up with the key cards.

Stephen took the stack and looked through it. 'Our machines should be able to read some of these. Others, I may need help with. I know a vendor who owes me a favor, but it could take some time to get hold of him.'

'That's fine,' Rachel said, heading out the door. 'Just have them done before I meet with my lawyer on Monday.'

'Well, I don't know . . .' Stephen started, but the door had glided closed behind his sister. He turned back to me. 'Guess I'll have them done,' he said with a shrug.

But I was still looking at the calendars and day-planners on the desk. The dog-eared pages of my life as I had once known it. Or, like Rachel had said, thought it to be.

'Do you need to keep all of these?' I asked, moving to pick up the top one.

Stephen came over to me. 'For Rachel's purposes, the last three years are really all I need. You can take the earlier ones, unless . . .' He stopped.

I looked up at him. 'Unless I want to know if Ted was cheating before that?' The day-planner in my hand was from the year Eric was born. 'I do wish I knew,' I said under my breath.

'So you want me to look back further?'

I smiled sheepishly. 'Actually, what I meant was that I wish I knew if I want to know.'

'Is wondering better than knowing?'

I smiled ruefully. 'Your sister asked something similar.'

Stephen laughed. 'My sister doesn't usually ask,' he said. 'She tells. She's like our mother that way.'

I was paging through the planner. 'February 4. Ultrasound

– 2 p.m.' I remembered the day like it was yesterday. Actually, I remembered it more clearly than yesterday. February 4 was the first time I saw Eric, albeit as a shadowy figure on a monitor. I asked the technician if it was OK that he looked like a tadpole. She'd laughed and reassured me it was.

Reassured me. Just me.

Ted had missed that appointment. He was away at a meeting. Tampa, if I wasn't mistaken. He'd been in Tampa a lot.

I had been holding my breath and now I let it out. Maybe it was time to let go of other things, too.

'That's fine,' I said, putting the calendar I'd been holding back on the desk. 'Go as far as you can.'

Stephen nodded, his brown eyes watchful, but he didn't say anything.

I knew that he was feeling sorry for me. It made me uncomfortable. I don't like people to pity me. It made me feel . . . pitiful.

'Assuming you have the time, of course.' I was trying to put both of us at ease. 'After all, you probably have better things to do than—'

Stephen waved aside the objection. 'Right now, I admit, I have to get to this meeting. But I'd be happy to do what I can after that.'

It seemed like a lot of work to do for a virtual stranger. 'That's very nice of you, but why?'

Stephen shrugged. 'Anything I find can only strengthen Rachel's argument and, in turn, protect the family.' All of a sudden he was looking as dignified as the office he stood in. It seemed an uncomfortable fit.

'*The Family?*' I asked, picking up my brown paper bag and flattening it. 'In capital letters?'

Stephen blushed. It went nicely with the tousled hair. 'Only the "T" and the "F".'

'What a relief,' I said, tucking the grocery bag under my arm. 'I'd hate to see you going all caps.'

He laughed. 'Self-aggrandizing, I agree. Sometimes, though, we fall into the trap of believing our own marketing.' He walked me to the door.

'Don't I know it. I spent nearly twenty years in public relations.' Before I told him the *rest* of my life's story, I pulled open the door. 'Just let me know when you're done with the calendars and I'll swing by to get them.'

'I'd be happy to drop them off at your coffeehouse, if you like,' he volunteered, looking down at me. Then his expression changed. 'I want to thank you. What you're doing for my sister is—'

'Yeah, well, maybe I'm doing it for me, too,' I said, slipping out into the elevator corridor.

Stephen Slattery followed me and pushed 'Down'. The elevator door opened immediately and I stepped in.

'Yeah, well, maybe I'm doing it for you, too,' he said softly, as the elevator door closed.

Four

If you've dated someone a few times and never quite had sex with him, is it cheating to have impure thoughts about another man?

Beats me.

As I drove west on Brookhill Road toward home, I gave Stephen Slattery some thought. The man was damned attractive. And I thought maybe he liked me, too, despite the fact he was five or so years younger than me. Or maybe *because* of the age difference. Maybe I had become a cougar and didn't realize it.

Nah.

I was acting like a fourteen-year-old, but it was hard for me to be sure of these things. Ted had been my first real love. So now, cut loose, I was the equivalent of a relationship virgin. A really old relationship virgin.

Which might explain why I had no idea where things were going with Pavlik.

I pulled into the 'right turn only' lane behind a Brookhills Barbie – expensive wardrobe, more shoes than she can wear, tall, beautiful and a little bit plastic. Oh, and she even comes with her own sports car!

The light turned red and Barbie stopped, apparently going straight. Meaning I'd have to wait for the light to change before I could turn right on to Poplar Creek Road. I checked the time. Nearly six. I didn't know where Pavlik wanted to go to dinner, but I thought it might require more than an Uncommon Grounds T-shirt and a pair of blue jeans.

Pavlik and I had been going out – as best as our respective schedules allowed – for nearly a year, but the relationship hadn't been . . . consummated. Every time we got close something would happen. Pavlik would be called out to a crime scene. The burglar alarm would go off at Uncommon Grounds. I would trip over Frank and break my nose.

You know, the usual things.

It had gotten to be a joke between us, but I was a little tired of laughing. And a lot frustrated.

A part of me – the part that was still fourteen – wondered whether Pavlik really wanted the relationship to develop or if he was just as happy to continue with the occasional dinner date.

Like tonight.

As the light changed, someone to my left blasted the horn. I turned to see Sarah in her lemon yellow 1975 Firebird, squeal around the corner and turn left to head home. Sarah's horn was a lot like Sarah. In your face and annoying, but she was *your* horn, damn it.

My phone was ringing and Frank was barking as I climbed the steps of my front porch.

At the sound of my key sliding into the lock, both sounds stopped and Frank let out a doggy version of 'huh?' before making for the door. Well-versed in things 'Frank', I waited for him to run full tilt headfirst into the door and bounce back before I peered in.

He was sitting back on his haunches looking dazed and a little betrayed.

'You OK?' I asked as I stepped in.

Skirting the offending door with a suspicious look, Frank greeted me with great enthusiasm and a fair amount of drool, the latter of which I managed to dodge.

'So did you take a message?' I asked, scratching him behind what felt like an ear as I leaned over to hit the 'Play' button on the answering machine.

'Maggy, this is Jake,' the tape said. 'Things have been crazy here and I've been running all day. Would you be terribly disappointed if I picked up takeout and we ate in?'

I sighed and picked up the phone.

After the events of the afternoon, I'd really been looking forward to a nice evening to put the world right again.

To think about me and Pavlik, not about Rachel and Ted. Or Ted and . . . whoever the 'her' was this time.

I knew all too well how Rachel was feeling, because I'd felt it, too, despite my attempts to explain it away to myself.

Ted had been different. Often distant, but then inexplicably overly charming. I'd thought maybe it was the business. He'd stopped talking to me about it, but I knew the dental practice didn't seem to be bringing in the money it had been. Expenses – Rachel's upkeep, as it turned out – were outpacing income, and every time I pressed him to talk about it, he'd get angry.

I knew something was wrong and I fully expected the other shoe to drop at some point. I just didn't realize that shoe would have a five-inch stiletto heel capable of piercing my heart.

Pavlik answered on the first ring. 'Jake Pavlik.'

'Hello, sheriff,' I said in my most seductive tone.

'Maggy, is that you? Do you need to cancel? It sounds like you have a cold.'

I was just so incredibly bad at this. Did anybody ask Mae West if that come-hither voice was the result of the sniffles? Or Kathleen Turner if that fine sheen of seductive sweat in *Body Heat* was caused by a fever?

I cleared my throat. 'No, I'm fine.'

'Good,' Pavlik said, 'because I'm really looking forward to seeing you tonight.'

Now that was more promising. 'Me, too, and takeout is good. Would you like me to pick it up, though, if you're pressed for time?'

'Nope. I need to run home to let Muffin out, anyway, and the restaurant is between our house and yours.'

Muffin is a pit bull that Pavlik rescued from a dog-fighting ring. Pudgy and devoid of teeth, Muffin was my greatest rival for Pavlik's affection. Even so, I loved the toothless little tub.

Muffin's dad sounded distracted and I could hear him shuffling through papers. 'Is there anything in particular you want?' he asked.

Yes, sheriff. Put down those papers and get over here and do me. But then I couldn't say that. 'You pick it,' I said instead.

'I'll see you in an hour.'

As often happens, lowered expectations led to higher rewards.

Pavlik arrived with two big bags of Asian fusion food. I didn't know if it was Chinese, Japanese, Thai, Vietnamese or Laotian, but it all looked fabulous.

'This is like a treasure hunt,' I said, eagerly opening cardboard box after cardboard box. 'Each one looks better than the last.'

Pavlik shook his head. 'If only I'd known the way to your heart was Asian food.'

He was smiling and his eyes looked cornflower blue. This was both a good sign and a bad sign. It meant he was happy, since Pavlik's eyes turned stormy as his emotions got stronger. Anger turned them dark gray, but then so did desire. At least I thought so, from the glimpses I'd gotten before the love train was derailed each time.

'Believe me, sheriff,' I said, picking up another box, 'this is only one way to my heart. Oooh, Kung Pao Chicken!'

Pavlik took the box away from me and set it on the coffee table. Then he pulled me closer to him on the couch. 'You know, I have other ways of making you squeal with delight.'

I snuggled in. He smelled of soap and aftershave. It was even better than Kung Pao Chicken. 'You do?'

'Yup, and I think I know where we've gone wrong.' He lifted my hair and kissed the back of my neck.

I gave a little quiver. 'Ohhhh . . . how?'

'Each time we have dinner and then, after dinner, just about when we get to this point –' Pavlik's lips moved down to that little notch by the collarbone – 'something happens.' He slid his hands up under my shirt, laying them flat against my stomach to pull me against him.

Something was happening all right. But I thought Pavlik meant something happened to *prevent* something from happening.

'It does,' I managed softly in his ear. 'So what do we do to fix that?' I nuzzled the lock of dark hair that fell over the top of his ear.

He lifted his head to look at me. His eyes were nearly black. 'We start with dessert.'

I *love* dessert.

At midnight we reheated the food.

'Where did we put the Kung Pao Chicken?' I asked as Frank padded into the kitchen.

The sheepdog burped.

'The coffee table,' Pavlik said, looking at Frank.

'Frank level,' I said sadly. 'Think he ate all of it?'

'Please don't tell me you're suggesting we finish off the rest,' Pavlik said, giving me a kiss on the nose. 'Even you can't love Kung Pao Chicken that much.'

'Actually, I was trying to gauge whether it would be wise to put him outside.'

Frank farted and then looked around to see who had done it.

'Whoa.' Pavlik waved his hand in front of his nose. 'That's ripe. I think outside and away from open flames is the way to go.'

'Agreed.' I tapped Frank on the head. 'Guess who's sleeping out tonight?'

Frank farted again and followed me to the front porch. The poor thing looked embarrassed.

When I came back in, Pavlik was spooning food from my mismatched microwave-safe dishes on to our plates. He looked positively domestic, except for the fact he was wearing nothing but his skivvies.

I snuck in between Pavlik and the kitchen counter, wrapped my arms around him and laid my head on his chest. He rested his head on the top of mine. 'I have an idea,' he murmured into my hair. 'Why don't we have dinner and then . . .'

'Dessert?' I supplied.

'Oh, yeah.'

*   *   *

The next morning was Sunday – heavens be praised.

There was a handsome man in my bed, a sheepdog on my porch, a Sunday newspaper at my front door and coffee brewing in the kitchen.

It was perfect.

Too perfect.

Pavlik's phone rang.

He kissed me before he flipped it open. We had been lying in bed, waiting for the coffee to finish before we made our way into the kitchen for sustenance.

'Pavlik.'

I watched as he listened, all business now. I couldn't make anything out from his eyes. In fact, they seemed to go blank. He glanced once toward me, then away again.

Something was wrong.

'So how long has it been?' he asked.

I could hear a voice on the other end, but couldn't make out any of the words, damn it.

'Not enough to be considered missing,' Pavlik was saying. 'But given the . . .' Listening again.

'OK, I'll meet you in the office in twenty minutes so you can brief me.'

He hung up and gave me a regretful look. 'I'm sorry. I have to—'

I put my hand over his mouth. 'You don't have to apologize. It sounded serious.'

Pavlik looked at me, considering. 'I guess I can tell you since you'll likely find out soon anyway. I understand the media has already been called.'

'About what?' I pulled the sheet up around me, suddenly cold, and not just because I'd been deprived of Pavlik's warmth.

He was up now, pulling on his clothes. 'About your ex-husband's new wife, Rachel Slattery. She didn't come home last night.'

Pavlik let Frank in as he left. As the front door closed, the sheepdog jumped up on the bed. He looked around and nosed under the pillow to make sure no one was hiding there. Then he settled down on to the bed, throwing me a reproachful look for allowing an interloper to besmirch 'our' bed.

'Sorry, boy,' I said, giving him a scratch. 'But God knows, it doesn't happen often.'

Frank farted.

'That's it,' I said. 'Off!' I pointed at the ground. Frank licked my finger, but didn't move.

No matter. I had bigger problems than a farting sheepdog.

Like a husband – excuse me, ex-husband – who was cheating on his new wife. And whose said wife was now missing. And to compound things even further, Rachel must have disappeared just hours after telling both me and her brother that she intended to prove Ted was cheating and then divorce him.

That couldn't bode well for Ted.

'But then, I'm not Ted,' I asserted.

Frank opened one eye and looked at me. Apparently agreeing, he went back to sleep.

This wasn't my problem, so why did I feel so awful?

I mean, besides the fact that I had started to like Rachel in a grudging kind of way.

The phone rang. The caller ID said 'X', my code for Ted.

'Can you come over here?' Ted asked before I had time to even say 'hello'. 'Something awful has happened. Rachel is missing.'

'I know,' I said automatically and then paused to censor myself. Did I really want Ted to know Pavlik had slept over?

Yes. 'I was with the sheriff when the call came in.' In bed. Naked.

No reaction.

'I'm sorry to be calling you,' Ted said. 'But I didn't know what else to do. I don't have anybody but Rachel. And Eric, of course, but I can't call him.' He sounded frantic. He sounded like he was going to cry.

The only time I'd seen Ted cry was when his dad died. I felt badly for him now, as I had then. But I was his ex-wife. His cheated upon ex-wife. 'Why don't you call your mother?' I suggested.

'She's in Berlin. Or maybe London.'

Martine Thorsen had become a bit of a jet-setter since her husband had died. The first trip was within two weeks of his death and I'd always had the sneaking suspicion that she hadn't considered her husband Thor, Ted's father, much of a loss. I wondered if Thor had been as much of a tomcat as his son was. Or is.

'Please, Maggy,' Ted pleaded. 'I really need you. The sheriff's department was here.'

The implication was that I had more experience in dealing with them than he did, and therefore should hop out of my warm bed and come to his aid.

I felt an overpowering urge to do just that, but I didn't think it was for Ted's sake or even for Rachel. No, I was willing to leave my warm bed because I was curious.

'Curiosity killed the tomcat,' I said out loud.

'What?' Ted asked on the other end. I didn't answer. I was too busy thinking. What could have happened last night? Despite what she'd told me, had Rachel decided to confront Ted with what she knew and leave? But Pavlik said she never came home.

I dislodged Frank. 'I'm on my way. Who else is there?'

'No one. I'm alone.'

'Shouldn't you call Rachel's family?'

'Her mother and father were here, but they left after they talked to the deputies. I think they're putting together some sort of reward.'

'What about Stephen?'

There was a hesitation. 'Stephen? You mean Rachel's brother? How do you know him?'

'We just met,' I said honestly, but didn't elaborate. 'Does he know about Rachel?'

'I talked to him on the phone. He sounded funny,' Ted said. 'It was like he thought I had something to do with Rachel's being gone. That's nuts.'

My mind might have been running a hundred miles an hour, but apparently my mouth wasn't quick enough for Ted.

'That's nuts, right?' he repeated.

'Right.' Unless Ted found out that Rachel knew he was cheating on her.

Ted was still yammering, but I wasn't listening to him in real-time. I was playing back the conversation I'd had with him yesterday. The one when I'd told him Rachel and I had talked. And that she'd said Ted had been 'busy'.

Busy. An innocuous word, but maybe not so innocuous if you were the 'busy' one and feeling guilty.

Had Ted gone home and asked Rachel about what she'd said to me?

Worse, had there been an argument, maybe a violent one?

Worst, had I *caused* all this?

Five

By the time I reached Ted and Rachel's home on Wildwood Drive, I'd calmed down a bit.

Fact was, I was just guessing at all this. I didn't have any proof that Ted was cheating on Rachel, much less that he'd been cheating on me with anyone besides Rachel. She couldn't have had any solid evidence either, or she wouldn't have come to see me yesterday.

I also had no way of knowing what Rachel had told Ted last night. In fact, I didn't even know if Rachel had seen Ted last night. She'd been on her way to a meeting at the Hamilton when she'd left Stephen's office. Had she made it there? Had she gone home after that?

I assumed that Stephen would tell the authorities – whether it was Pavlik or someone else – about my visiting his office with Rachel. What I didn't know was how much detail he would give them. It put me in an awkward position. The last thing I wanted to do was get tangled up in another one of Pavlik's investigations. Especially when things were finally heating up between us.

I edged my Escape past a dark blue Miata parked to the side on the driveway and stopped near the house. As I had the two or three other times I'd come here to pick up Eric, I tried not to compare the pink brick mini-mansion with my post-divorce mini- . . . well, just mini. And as if Ted and Rachel's house wasn't already big enough, it looked like the brush to one side had been being cleared for an addition of some sort.

As I trudged up the driveway toward the front door, it opened and a yapping chihuahua came squirting out.

Finally, one area where mine was bigger than theirs.

Frank could have sat on ChiChi the chihuahua and not even noticed. Not that Frank was exactly Princess and the Pea material. Once I'd found him sound asleep on the front steps, rump on the porch, head on the sidewalk below. I guess when you're tired, you're tired.

ChiChi didn't look like she *got* tired. She was dancing around in circles like a crazed wind-up toy. Ted followed her out.

My ex-husband was wearing gray sweatpants and a Bucky Badger sweatshirt from the University of Wisconsin, our alma mater. His hair was more bedhead than the artfully unstyled look he'd sported since Rachel had gotten hold of him and introduced him to gel. Or it would have looked like bedhead, if I thought for a moment he had gone to sleep. His nose was red, his eyes sunken.

If this was an act, it was a really good one.

But then, I reminded myself as I mounted the steps to the big front door, a man who juggles two or maybe three women for two years better be pretty damn good at lying.

'Any word?' I asked as I reached him.

Ted shook his head. 'Nothing.' He stepped back through the doorway, whistling for ChiChi. The chihuahua and I padded in after him.

I closed the door and paused to look around. The house was as I remembered it. Unlike the Slattery Arms with its heavy brocades and jewel tones, Rachel and Ted's house was light and airy. Both the foyer and the living room beyond were painted that mustardy color – Amy would know the name of it – that rightfully should look awful but managed to achieve charming and sophisticated.

Rachel's touch, no doubt. If she weren't missing, I'd probably have to hate her for being so good at something I had no talent for. Now I could only feel guilty. Not only for being jealous of her, but for what I might have done that may have contributed to her disappearance.

I hadn't said much to Ted the afternoon before, but if he already was wary of being caught cheating, it might have been enough to alert him that Rachel was on to him.

I found Ted in his chair in the living room. I knew that

it was his chair, because it had lived in my house for many years. Ted had built the sling chair of stained two-by-fours in college. The sling between the head and foot of the chair held two cushions. They were covered in flowered chintz now, but in college it had been Wisconsin Badger red. I'd sewed them myself and Ted and I had filled them with foam stuffing as we watched Badger football on TV.

We usually lost back then, but at the end of each game the marching band would take the field and the students would leap up and stomp to the music, making the upper deck of the stadium sway. Then, finally, the players would burst back out of the locker room to dance with the band.

Win or lose.

Good times or bad.

That was youth.

That was resiliency.

And probably a whole lot of beer.

I looked at Ted, who had his head in his hands. 'Something to drink?'

He sighed. 'I want a beer, but I'll have coffee.'

'Coffee it is.' Coffee I could do. I was good at coffee. And I really needed a cup myself. I hadn't thought to grab a cup on the way out of the house.

No worries. Rachel had one of those great single-cup brewing pots, where you slip in the pouch filled with coffee, flavored or not, and voila, you have coffee. If we had a couple of them in the store, we could just hand customers their individual packets when they walked in and have them brew their own.

Might work. People went to restaurants, picked out their steaks and grilled them themselves, for God's sake. Pretty soon they'd be paying extra for the privilege of butchering the steer.

As I waited for the cup to fill, I looked around Rachel's kitchen. I was feeling guilty for being there. I wasn't sure why. Much as I had hated her for 'stealing Ted', as I had thought of it, I'd tried to take the high road. Which meant I thought really horrible things, but didn't say them. At least to her.

And yesterday I'd been more than nice. In fact, I'd actually started to like the little slut. Even agreed to help her
catch others of her species.

The pot beeped and I took Ted's cup out from under the
filter and inserted another for me. Then I switched out the
bundle of soggy grounds for a new one. Hazelnut cream
sounded good.

I added one Splenda and a little cream and took Ted's
cup to him before it got cold.

He looked up as I held it out to him. 'What am I going
to do, Maggy?'

'I don't know,' I said, giving up any thoughts of going
back to the kitchen for my coffee immediately. I sat down
on the couch across from him. 'Why don't you tell me what
you've already done.'

I wasn't quite sure what I was asking him, but it sounded
like one of those great open-ended questions they ask on TV.

Ted shrugged, looking away from me, but didn't say
anything.

'You called the sheriff's department, right?' I prodded.

'First, I called her house – I mean, her parents' house –
thinking maybe she was there.'

'When?' I asked. 'This morning?'

Ted looked startled. 'No, last night at about nine.'

'So she didn't come home at all last night?' I was trying
to put a timeline together in my head. Rachel had left
Stephen's office a little after three o'clock toward a three
thirty meeting at the Hamilton.

'Do you know where she went after her meeting at the
Hamilton?' I asked before I could think of all the reasons
I probably shouldn't.

'What meeting?' Ted had taken a sip of the coffee and
was holding the cup lop-sided, the hot liquid threatening
to spill.

I took the cup away from him and set it on a coaster on
the cherry table next to him. Maybe I was being considerate. Then again, maybe I was buying time to figure out
how to answer.

How much should I, or shouldn't I, tell Ted about yesterday

afternoon's events? It would all come out eventually, though later seemed a whole lot better than sooner right now. Especially since Rachel might have her own reasons for taking off for a while.

Besides, if Ted didn't know what Rachel had been up to, my tipping him off would not endear me to law enforcement. Especially Pavlik. And I really, really wanted to keep being . . . endeared by him.

'I told you I saw Rachel yesterday,' I reminded Ted. 'She said you both had been very busy.' There. I'd covered myself on what I'd let slip the previous afternoon. 'She was on her way to a three thirty meeting at the Hamilton.'

'That's great,' Ted said, leaping to his feet. 'You have to tell the sheriff. It will give them someplace to start looking.'

'I figured Stephen . . .' I slapped my mouth closed, but it was too late.

'Stephen Slattery? I thought you just met him.' If I didn't know better, I would have thought Ted sounded jealous.

Think quick, Maggy. I jumped up. 'Wait! I think I hear my coffee!' I ran out of the room.

Fortunately, I'd forgotten to push the brew button, so that bought me a few extra seconds. *Un*fortunately, Ted got impatient and came in after me.

'What does Stephen have to do with this?' he asked.

The smell of brewing coffee had settled me down a bit. The answer to the question was obvious. 'Stephen was with Rachel when I saw her,' I said as the coffee machine beeped, signaling it was finished brewing.

'Oh.' Ted reached for the freshly brewed cup. My cup. My hazelnut cream cup. Before I could stop him, he tore open a packet of Splenda and dumped it in. 'So if Rachel went with Stephen, he'd know when they left the Hamilton.'

'He didn't go with her.' I watched Ted dump in cream. Way too much cream.

'Why wouldn't he go with her?' Ted asked, taking a sip and pulling out a chair, as if to sit. 'He's the executive VP of Slattery Hotels, not Rachel. She couldn't have cared less about the hotel business.'

'That's all you know,' I muttered. I needed coffee. I'd

left home without it and now I'd been aced out of it here. I was getting cranky. I stuck another cup under the brewer. 'Rachel told me she was getting involved in the family business. She said it was time she stepped up.'

Ted looked genuinely astonished. 'But that's ridiculous. Why now, when—'

Ted was interrupted by ChiChi, who came skittering around the corner into the kitchen. Using the pulled-out kitchen chair as a ramp, he launched himself at Ted.

Startled, Ted dropped the coffee cup and it hit the floor, shattering. 'What the hell?'

'Doorbell. Wait for it.'

He looked at me.

'The doorbell is going to ring in a second,' I explained. 'Dogs sense it.'

Sure enough. *Bling. Bling.*

No pedestrian 'ding-dong' for Rachel's house.

I looked at the mess on the floor and did a cost-benefit analysis of answering the bell versus cleaning up the mess. 'I'll get the door,' I offered.

Pulling the heavy front door open, I fully expected to see a cadre of Slatterys.

Instead I found a cadre of . . . Pavlik.

He looked at me. I looked at him. Neither of us seemed thrilled to see the other one.

'Hi,' I said lamely.

'Hi.' His eyebrows worked their way down his forehead from the heights they'd achieved when he saw me to the depths they typically reached when he was ticked at me.

'Didn't I just leave you in bed?' Pavlik signaled for the deputy standing by his squad car to wait outside and stepped in.

'Ted called me. He was frantic.'

Pavlik didn't say anything. He's good at this sheriff stuff.

'His mother is in Berlin. Or London.' I said it like it explained everything. 'To tell you the truth, I was surprised you weren't here when I arrived.'

It was a little fib, since Ted had told me no one was there.

'I stopped at the department.' Pavlik was moving deeper

into the house as he spoke, heading toward the living room.

'Isn't everyone jumping the gun?' I asked, trailing after him. 'Maybe Rachel just decided to go away for a while.' I said the last part as I maneuvered to get between Pavlik and the living room.

Pavlik glanced in at Ted, who was back in his chintz sling chair. My ex-husband had hold of ChiChi and was stroking him like his life depended on it. Ted's, not the dog's. The chihuahua looked unenthusiastic, at best. At worst, he looked like he was going to take off one of Ted's fingers with those tiny, razor-sharp teeth.

Pavlik turned back to me. 'Maybe she just went away?'

'Women need to do that sometimes,' I asserted, like I was some sort of an expert on the habits of the female species. Fact is, I scarcely understood myself, much less anyone else. 'Sometimes we need to go,' I hesitated, 'umm . . . to a spa.'

Pavlik looked at me. 'Have you ever been to a spa?'

'No, but I don't have all this either.' I waved my hand toward the living room. 'It must be very . . . stressful.'

As if on cue, there was a crash. I looked in on Ted. The first cup of coffee, the one I'd set on the end table, was on the floor and Ted was standing, holding his thumb. ChiChi was nowhere in sight. Having apparently bitten the hand that feeds him, he'd made a break for it.

'You seem awfully eager to protect him,' Pavlik said, nodding toward Ted.

I didn't like the way this was going. I'd had a spectacular time with Pavlik last night and I had no intention of ruining it. I also had no desire to protect Ted. I looked over at my former spouse, who was trying to stem the flow of blood by wiping his thumb on his sweatshirt.

'Protect him?' I asked. 'The man doesn't need a protector. He needs a nanny.'

I almost got a smile from Pavlik. At the very least, his face softened. 'You need to stay out of this one, Maggy, for your own sake. There's more going on here than you know.' He touched my arm. 'Than you want to know.'

As much as I aspired to be a strong, independent woman,

I was a sucker for being taken care of. Must be all those years of taking care of other people.

I stepped back and Pavlik entered the living room. He stuck out his hand to Ted and I belatedly realized the two had never met. 'I'm Sheriff Jake Pavlik. And you are?'

Of course Pavlik knew who Ted was. He was standing in Ted's house, after all. I recognized the technique, unfortunately, from when Pavlik had interviewed me the first time we met. The man had a way of making you feel like an insignificant bug. Even in your own house – or coffeehouse.

It did work wonders, though. 'Ted Thorsen,' my ex said, sticking out his hand. There was still blood dripping off the thumb. The damned dog must be a vampire.

The two men shook lefty, while I ducked into the kitchen to get something to mop up.

'Here,' I said, returning and handing Ted a paper towel. Pavlik ignored me. I suspected he was letting me stay for the same reason a miner keeps a canary. My reaction might let him know whether Ted was gassing him or not.

'Ted Thorsen,' Pavlik said, pulling out his notebook. 'I thought I saw here that your name was . . .' He thumbed through the pages until he found the one he wanted and then looked up. 'Tor?'

Ted's ears turned red.

'His parents' names are Martine and Thor,' I piped in.

Ted shot me a look.

I shrugged. 'Just trying to explain it's not your fault.'

Ted's father and I had waged a nine-month battle about Eric's name. Thor had wanted Canute. I won. I was half Norwegian, too, but I preferred normal names like Simon or Eric. You know, the ones from *my* side of the family.

'OK,' Pavlik said, 'so Tor Thorsen.'

I giggled.

Now both of them shot me dirty looks. 'I'm sorry,' I pleaded. 'It's just been a while since I've heard it.' I waved my hands. 'I'm fine now.'

Pavlik just nodded. The man was made of ice.

'Have you heard something from Rachel?' Ted asked eagerly. 'Maggy says—'

By that time, Pavlik had heard enough of what 'Maggy' had to say. He cut Ted off. 'No, we haven't.'

He was leafing through the notebook again. 'Your wife's family provided us with some interesting information, though. Something that you didn't seem to think was important enough to share.'

Uh-oh. Here it comes. I looked down at my feet and only then realized I had two different sneakers on. Not that it mattered. It was all going to come out now. Ted's cheating on Rachel. Rachel's visit to me. Our visit to Stephen. The possible reason for Rachel's disappearance.

'You see, that's what I meant,' I said, trying to get out ahead of it. 'Rachel was probably just upset and that's why she took off for the night.'

Pavlik looked uncertainly at me, a rare crack in his interview-armor. Then, gathering himself, he turned back to Ted.

'*Was* your wife upset, Mr Thorsen? Or was it *you* who was upset that she was pregnant?'

Six

'Pregnant?' I turned toward Ted. There was no reason it should have hurt, but it did. There was no reason I should have cared, but . . . I did.

'I'm really sorry, Maggy,' Ted said. 'I should have told you.'

'Don't be silly.' I had to stop to clear my throat. I was trying to sound normal, but probably not fooling anyone. 'There's no reason to apologize. I'm happy for you. Congratulations.' I plastered a happy-smile on my face.

Pavlik was just watching, willing to see how it all played out.

'Still, you always—' Ted started to say, but I interrupted, already embarrassed enough by my reaction.

'You can't imagine that I want another baby. I mean, Eric is eighteen, for God's sake. I'm closer to being a grand-mother than a mother.'

I got it then. I knew why I was reacting the way I was. The issue wasn't having a baby or not. It was moving on or not. Ted had a new wife and a new baby on the way. Me? I was standing still. No, I was doing worse than standing still. Ted was getting younger and I was getting . . . old. Suddenly I knew how Caron felt.

Ted was patting me on the shoulder. 'You are not old enough to be a grandmother. You look fantastic,' he said reassuringly. Or was it patronizingly? Guess it depended on my mood.

I waved him off, glancing self-consciously at Pavlik. My lover. Once. Before I was old enough to be a grandmother.

'I think we have more important things to think about here,' I said. 'For example, when was the last time you saw Rachel?'

Ted, taken aback, looked at Pavlik.

Pavlik shrugged. 'Answer the question.'

'Yesterday morning when I left for the office,' Ted said and then turned the tables on me. 'And you said you saw her and Stephen yesterday afternoon, right? And that Rachel was on her way to a meeting at the Hamilton?'

Pavlik looked surprised, but I just nodded.

'Why didn't Stephen say anything to me about it on the phone?' Ted said.

'Maybe he assumed you knew,' I offered. 'That Rachel told you.'

I looked at Pavlik. For the moment the sheriff appeared content to let us interview ourselves. And it seemed to be working.

'I didn't know anything about any meeting,' Ted said. 'Rachel said she was going to spend her day shopping for furniture for the nursery we're adding.' Ted's voice broke.

The prep work I had seen outside must be for the nursery. Here I was worrying about growing old and Ted was hoping both Rachel and her baby would have a chance to do the same.

Pavlik flipped the cover closed on his notebook and slid it into his coat pocket. 'We'll call you when we know something,' he said to Ted. 'I assume you'll be around?'

Recognizing the signs, I led the way to the door.

'Of course,' Ted said, trailing behind Pavlik.

'I'm going to see Stephen Slattery,' Pavlik said to me as I stopped in the foyer. 'Then I'll want to talk to you. Will you be home?'

'Either there or at Uncommon Grounds,' I said, opening the door. 'But I don't—' I looked out and felt like Dorothy when she steps out of the farmhouse after the cyclone. We weren't in Kansas anymore.

But wherever we were, it must be a slow news day.

Three microwave news trucks were parked on the street and two more were just pulling up. News people were piling out of the vehicles, the reporters standing impatiently with their microphones as the camera operators unpacked equipment and hoisted cameras on to their shoulders.

One reporter, a dark-haired woman, caught sight of us and started to sprint up the driveway in her ruby red Jimmy Choos. That started a stampede of people, cameras and wires.

I tried to close the door, but the brunette reporter stuck her foot in. I wouldn't have hesitated slamming the door on a pair of loafers, but the Jimmy Choos made me hesitate long enough for her to push a microphone in my face.

'Who are you?' she demanded. 'And why are you here?'

Before I could have answered, even if I'd wanted to, her question was followed by a dozen more shouted by other reporters who had no more idea who I was than she did. Nonetheless, they figured I knew something and they weren't above talking over each other to find out what that was.

'When was the last time you saw—'

'I understand a reward has been offered for inform—'

'Was there any indication from her behavior that—'

'Ladies and gentlemen!'

Everyone went quiet.

'You are on private property,' Pavlik continued, moving out on to the porch. 'If you'll follow me to the street, I'll give you a statement.'

He turned to me and to Ted, who was standing just out of sight. 'Shut the door and lock it. If anyone steps on the property, call the department. We'll arrest them for trespassing.'

Pavlik started down the sidewalk, most of the reporters following. As I went to close the door, though, the dark-haired woman gave it another try. 'Who did you say you were?' she demanded.

'I didn't.' I started to swing the door closed, but she stuck her foot in again.

This time I didn't let the Choo sway me, but kept on swinging. She pulled out just in time, but as the door closed, the edge of it caught the heel and popped the shoe off. It landed inside.

I locked the door and eyed the shoe.

'You can't keep it, you know,' Ted said as the pounding started up on the other side of the door.

'But it's so pretty,' I said wistfully.

'Open up,' the woman yelled.

'There's only one of them,' Ted pointed out.

'I'd put it on a table and admire it.' God knows I would never be able to afford to buy two of them. I picked up the shoe and balanced it on the palm of my hand. 'Look at it. It's beautiful. It should be in a museum, not on some news-munchkin's foot.'

Ted gave me a strange look. 'Well, it belongs to the . . . munchkin. You have to give it back.'

More pounding.

I sighed. He was right.

I opened the door and held out my hand. 'Take your Choo and get out,' I said.

The woman grabbed the shoe, threw me a furious look and hobbled down the walkway to where her camera operator was waiting in the cluster around Pavlik.

I closed the door.

'I can see why you'd like the sheriff,' Ted said to me as we walked back to the kitchen. 'He's the assertive type.'

Which Ted wasn't, was the unspoken part of his comment and he was right. I'd always had to make all the decisions in the family. It was nice to have someone suggest picking up something for dinner. Or having dessert.

I hoped I'd have dessert again. Sometime.

I looked at the broken cup – the first one – still on the kitchen floor. I felt like I'd spent my whole life cleaning up other people's messes.

Now Rachel was missing. And she was pregnant. The pregnancy added a whole new dimension to what was already a bad situation.

There had been a rash of similar stories in the news over the last couple of years. Young wife goes missing – young *pregnant* wife – leaving behind a frantic husband. A husband who later turns out to have murdered his 'beloved' spouse.

According to Amy, fount of all knowledge, homicide is one of the leading causes of death for pregnant women in the US. She said as many as twenty percent of the women who die during pregnancy are murder victims. Staggering.

I looked at Ted crouched on the floor, clumsily trying to pick up the broken pieces of cup. ChiChi wanted in on the action and Ted kept moving the dog aside.

Could this man have hurt his pregnant wife?

I didn't know. But what I did know was that he was cheating on her. And had cheated on me, maybe with more than one woman. I had gone years without knowing. Without even suspecting.

'You're going to get those teensy-weensy feet of yours cut, if you don't watch out,' Ted was saying gently to the dog.

ChiChi stuck out his little pink tongue and licked Ted on the nose.

Could dogs tell the good guys from the bad?

I hoped so, because I'd sure as hell proved that I couldn't.

Calling to Ted that he should let me know when he heard something, I snuck a peek out the front door. The media were still there, but at least they were following Pavlik's orders to stay off the property. I slipped out the door and made a dash for the Escape.

I wasn't fooling anyone. By the time I got to the SUV, the video cameras were up and focused and the still cameras had joined them and were snapping wildly. I started the Escape and put it in reverse, backing carefully down the driveway so as not to hit either the swarming reporters or the Miata parked in the driveway.

The Miata triggered a memory. Ted and I had gone out immediately and bought a minivan when we found out I was pregnant. It had seemed urgent, like the seven-pound baby couldn't possibly fit in our Alliance Hatchback on the way home from the hospital.

Yesterday afternoon, Rachel had been driving a new, super-sized SUV, not a pretty little sports car like the Miata. I should have tipped to it. By now SUVs probably had edged out minivans as the most popular family vehicles. I was willing to bet the Escalade was a recent purchase in preparation for the baby.

I backed out on to the street, ignoring the shouted questions as the reporters rallied round the car. I put the Escape in drive and moved forward steadily. As I did, I saw my Jimmy Choo reporter, now wearing both shoes, put a hand on her camera operator's arm to move him aside as I passed.

'The bitch will run you over,' I heard her say, even with my windows rolled up tight.

Damn right.

The sea of reporters parted in front of me. Despite what my mom told me in high school, having a bad reputation could be a very good thing.

I drove a couple of blocks away, parked the car and sat.

So Rachel was going to have a baby.

I'd always been good at guessing that a friend was pregnant before she announced it, but this one had gotten right past me.

Rachel had been pretty shrewd yesterday afternoon, if you thought about it. When I'd offered her a drink, she'd asked for a mimosa. If Ted had told her anything about our wedding, Rachel knew that I can't – or perhaps, shouldn't – drink champagne.

Given that, a request for a mimosa in my house would be a pretty low percentage bet. Add the fact you also need a caffeine-free beverage like orange juice to mix with it and the chances are slim to none.

Then Rachel had asked for white Zinfandel, the 'starter wine' that she would rightly figure the 'starter wife', who thought she knew something about wine, would look down her nose at.

I'd messed her up on that one, though, with my faux white Zin. She'd barely taken a sip, though – that I'd noticed. And she could very well have faked even that.

Rachel didn't want me to know she was pregnant. Why?

The most obvious reason was that it was none of my business. Admittedly, though, my calendars were none of *her* business and that didn't seem to bother her much.

Then again, Rachel might have been being sensitive to my feelings, thinking I would be upset at the thought of Ted starting another family. Still, a baby on the way would have strengthened her argument for the calendars. I was surprised she hadn't used it to get my sympathy.

I was probably over-thinking this. Maybe Rachel didn't feel like she was far enough along to tell people. I'd certainly seen no sign of a baby bump and a lot of expectant women don't announce their pregnancy until after the first trimester, when the greatest chance of miscarriage is past.

A baby.

It was true that Ted hadn't wanted another child. Eric was enough he had said.

And he was. In fact, during the eighteen months the colicky baby hadn't slept through the night, not even once, Eric had been more than enough for both of us to handle. Having barely survived that period and a full time job, I had been OK with calling it a day, conceptually-speaking.

But Rachel was young. It would make sense that she'd want a family. Had Ted? I didn't have a clue.

I started the car and pulled away from the curb.

From Wildwood, I turned north on to Poplar Creek Drive, which, as you might guess, parallels Poplar Creek. The creek runs north and south through Brookhills County.

Ted and Rachel's neighborhood, Wildwood Highlands, is the newest, most expensive development in the area. It's on the far south end of Poplar Creek Drive – so far that half the subdivision isn't even in the town proper, though still in Brookhills County. That fact had caused some magnificent arguments at the town hall and the courthouse over things like sewer and water, trash collection, school districts and, of course, taxes.

Big houses, big taxes – what town wouldn't want a piece of that? Brookhills certainly did, which is why there was talk of annexing the land and making it part of the town.

From Wildwood, the neighborhoods got less contentious and pretentious as you worked your way upstream. Not that there was anything wrong with them, but if you wanted people to know how much money you had, you headed downstream.

Me? I was upstream, pretty much as far as you could go.

Sandra Balzo

Even the salmon would have a hard time getting there. And if they did, they probably wouldn't stay to spawn.

Which made it all the more curious that Sarah Kingston, the most unpretentious of Brookhillians, lived just one step down – or in this case, upstream – from Ted and Rachel.

Sarah lived in fashionable Brookhills Estates with her two teenage charges, Sam and Courtney. When Patricia Harper, our former partner in Uncommon Grounds, had died last year, Sarah had stepped in as the kids' guardian. It had shocked all of us, but Sam and Courtney seemed to like it just fine. So did Sarah, though she didn't often admit it.

As I approached the entrance to Brookhills Estates, I made a quick decision and turned in. It was eleven a.m. on a Sunday. Maybe I'd find Sarah at home before she left to do an open house, or whatever real estate people had to do on Sunday afternoons.

Thing was, I didn't want to go home. My only other choice besides Sarah's house was Uncommon Grounds, where I'd be arriving right in time for the after-church crush. No, best to brave Sarah in the morning than the God-fearing in search of caffeine.

Sarah's house was a Painted Lady, a beautiful Victorian-style home painted in delicate shades of cream and rose. It's about as unSarah-like as anything you could imagine.

But then, Sarah had always been full of surprises and one of those surprises was walking out the front door.

Sarah. In a tennis skirt.

I gasped.

Sarah dropped her racket and her bag. 'Jesus, Maggy, you scared me. What's wrong with you?'

'What's wrong with *me*? What's wrong with you?'

I'd never seen Sarah in a skirt. Or a dress. In fact, if I was put on the witness stand, I couldn't even swear she had legs. I'd never actually seen them.

And, yet, here Sarah was, going off to play tennis like a regular Brookhills Barbie.

'You're playing tennis,' I accused her.

'No shit, Sherlock.' Sarah reached down to retrieve her racket. 'No wonder that sheriff keeps you around, if you're this good at deducing things. Which reminds me, has he de-dooed you, yet?'

'None of your business,' I said automatically. I was still trying to get used to the new anatomically correct Sarah. Who knew she actually had a waist and a pair of sturdy legs under the baggy pants outfits she'd been wearing.

But Sarah was looking me over as closely as I was examining her. 'You did. You had sex with Pavlik.'

I started to deny it, but why? God knows how long it would be before I had another chance at locker room bravado now that I was old enough to be a grandmother. 'Maybe.'

Sarah cackled and suddenly she seemed like her old self, despite the tennis togs. 'Well it's damn well time.' She tucked her racket in the tennis bag and slung the bag over her shoulder. 'I want to hear everything, but I'm meeting Emma for tennis at eleven thirty.'

Emma. Ted's ex-classmate and current running partner. Sarah's dentist and fitness guru. And perhaps the 'trois' in Ted and Rachel's 'ménage'?

'Really? Can I come along?'

Sarah looked startled. 'You want to watch me play tennis?'

'Of course. It's a beautiful spring day . . .' I paused to make sure, since I hadn't paid much attention up to now. Sure enough – sun shining, birds singing. 'I'd love to see you play.'

Sarah just looked at me.

'And support you,' I added.

Still nothing.

'In your fitness efforts,' I concluded.

She put down her tennis bag and folded her arms.

'OK, OK,' I said, holding my hands up in surrender. My God, the woman was a bully.

I ticked things off on my fingers as I went.

'One: my ex-husband's new wife, Rachel, caught him cheating.

'Two: she came to me yesterday afternoon for my help in proving Ted was cheating on her when he was married to me.

'Three: I finally agreed and we went to meet her good-looking brother.

'Four: Rachel went to a meeting and never came home last night.

'Five: Pavlik was called away from my house before we had breakfast.

'Six: Ted telephoned and asked me to come over.

'Seven: I was stupid and agreed.

'Eight: Pavlik arrived and found me there.

'Nine: and promptly announced that Rachel is pregnant.'

I held up my hands with nine fingers extended. 'Oh, and ten –' I unfolded the thumb – 'I want to come with you because I think your tennis partner may be the other woman.'

Sarah shrugged. 'Good enough.' She picked up her bag and signaled for me to follow.

Seven

It was a huge relief to unload on Sarah.

Usually, I don't tell people my bad news. I'd like to say that I wanted to spare them, but the truth is I'm sparing myself. Saying something – especially something bad – makes it real to me.

In this case, laying it all out in shorthand form to Sarah *had* made it real, but it also made it seem less like a nightmare, which I guess is the same thing. Real life we can deal with. Nightmares, well, we just hope to wake up.

The other problem with sharing things is that it subjects me to people's opinions, which I mostly don't want to hear. Unless they agree with mine.

Sarah, even in tennis togs, is totally insensitive, relentlessly honest and unnervingly free with her opinions. What makes her different than most people is that she really doesn't give a shit whether you take her advice.

'I can't do that,' I protested.

'Suit yourself.'

We had arrived at the tennis court and Sarah was busy unpacking her bag. Water bottle. Can of balls. Towel. Sunscreen. Sunglasses. Sweatband.

'It's just that with his sister missing and all . . .'

'Listen,' Sarah said, popping open the can of balls. 'You want to know what, if anything, Stephen Slattery told Pavlik. So ask Slattery.'

'But he's—'

'Hot,' Sarah supplied. 'Which is why you're afraid to approach him. It has nothing to do with your being considerate.'

I think I resented that. 'I feel like it would be going behind Pavlik's back.'

Sarah was squeezing a ball now, like she could tell if it was good. Everything I believed in would be destroyed if she actually could. 'Fine. So when Pavlik asks, tell him exactly what Rachel told you.'

'That Ted is a no-good cheating bastard and she was trying to uncover evidence that proved it so she could divorce him and he'd get nothing from her rich family?'

'Yeah, that's it.' Sarah gave up with the squeezing and started with the bouncing.

I grabbed the ball. 'But I was married to Ted for nearly twenty years. I've talked to Rachel a grand total of an hour in my lifetime. I'm going to take her word against Ted's?'

'Ted's word?' Sarah laughed. 'How can you say that with a straight face? He lied to you and cheated on you. That's why you divorced him, remember?'

What I remembered was *Ted* asking *me* for a divorce, so he could marry Rachel. I hadn't had a whole lot of say in the matter.

'You would have divorced him, you know.' It was like Sarah could read my mind sometimes. 'If he hadn't gotten out first, you would have kicked him out for fooling around.'

'Maybe,' I said. 'But if he'd confessed to the affair and promised it wouldn't happen again?' I shrugged. 'Who knows?'

Sarah took the ball out of my hand. '*I* know. You're not that stupid.'

At least one of us knew that.

'Thanks.' I lowered my voice because a figure was walking toward us from the parking lot. I assumed it was Emma. 'But if you dislike Ted so much, why do you go running with him?'

'I run with Emma.' Sarah nodded toward the attractive dark-haired woman approaching us. 'Ted comes along, that's fine. I don't have to like people or trust them to associate with them. I'm a real estate agent, for God's sake,' she hissed as she turned to greet Emma.

Even close up, Emma Byrne was still as attractive as I'd

remembered. Jet black hair, now shot with some gray. Dark blue eyes and an athletic body. She was just the woman Ted would choose to fool around with, if he didn't have a blonde-haired version at home, nearly twenty years younger.

'Maggy Thorsen,' Emma said, setting down her bag and sticking out her hand. 'It's been a long time. Great to see you.'

'Same here, Emma.' I pointed at Sarah, who had already moved away from us and was on the court. 'I understand you're the one to thank for the new Sarah.'

'She's still the same old Sarah, I think. Snarls at me no end when I call her to run or play tennis. I have to give her credit, though, she's keeping it up.' She cocked her head. 'You're looking good yourself. I understand you and the sheriff are an item.'

I smiled. 'I try to stay in shape.'

It was true. I did try. Just didn't succeed as much as I'd like.

Emma grinned. 'Not going to answer about the sheriff, huh? I don't blame you.' She pulled her racket out of her bag and pounded the strings against the palm of her hand. 'I'd keep him to myself, too.'

With that, she went to meet Sarah on the court. Me, I sat back to watch, not feeling nearly as old as I had an hour ago.

Sarah and Emma played two sets, with Emma winning both of them. Sarah did really well, though I did wonder whether Emma was taking it a bit easy on her.

'Do you play?' Emma asked when they were done.

'In college,' I admitted. 'But I haven't picked up a racket in about twenty years.'

'It's like riding a bike,' Emma said. 'Call me sometime.'

'I will. Or why don't you stop by the coffeehouse when you're at the clinic?'

Emma hesitated. 'Coffeehouse?'

'Uncommon Grounds. I own it.' So much for everyone knowing everything about everyone in Brookhills. Then again, Emma didn't live in Brookhills, she only worked there a few days a month.

She squinted at me. 'I could swear I've met the owner. Caron something?'

'Caron Egan. She's my partner.'

Emma blinked. 'Wow. That's quite a departure for you, isn't it? I thought you did PR for some bank.' She zipped her racket into its cover. 'What happened?'

'A moment of insanity,' I admitted. 'Owning your own business is tough.'

'Tell me about it,' she picked up her bag. 'That's why I threw in with the Dental Group. They own the clinics, equipment and all, so that eliminates the overhead and a lot of the headaches. I keep telling Ted he should think about it.'

She said it easily, without a trace of self-consciousness or subterfuge. As if she and Ted were simply friends. If they were having an affair, she was good. Of course, she'd had lots of years to practice.

'So? What do you think?' Sarah asked as we watched Emma walk away.

'I like her.'

'Yeah, me, too.' Sarah stuffed her racket into her bag. 'Still think she and Ted might be having an affair?'

'Sure.' I rubbed my forehead. 'Or they're just old friends. Your guess is as good as mine. Want to get coffee?'

'Quiet afternoon?' I asked when we walked into Uncommon Grounds.

Caron had a coffee pot in her hand. She turned, looked at us and gave a little shriek.

I glanced over at Sarah. 'The tennis skirt.'

Sarah nodded.

Amy came out from in back. 'Sarah, you have legs. Cool.'

She moved behind the espresso machine, hand poised above the portafilter, like a gunslinger getting ready to draw. 'What can I get you?'

The portafilter is a small wire mesh filter attached to a handle. To make an espresso, you fill it with finely ground French roast or espresso and tamp it down lightly, then you twist it on to the espresso machine, push a button and, presto! Espresso.

'Large skim latte,' I said. 'Sarah?'

'Same,' Sarah said.

I looked at her. 'You drink black coffee. The older the better.'

'That's when I smoked,' Sarah said, climbing on to a stool. 'Now I can taste things.'

'Want a shot of caramel in it?' Amy asked.

Sarah hesitated.

'We have sugar-free,' I told her and she nodded.

I was starting to understand the whole exercise thing. Sarah had quit smoking, which could make you pick up weight in and of itself. Plus, she was enjoying the taste of food, so she was tempted to eat more. Sarah wasn't just exercising to get healthy. She was exercising not to get fat. I was feeling ever so much better.

Amy poured two espresso shots in a latte mug and added a shot of sugar-free caramel. Meanwhile, she was steaming skim milk up to 180 degrees in a stainless steel frothing pitcher.

Holding back the froth with a spoon, she poured the hot milk into the latte and then topped it with a dollop of froth. A perfect caramel latte.

Meanwhile, Caron had recovered from the shock of Sarah's outfit. 'Can I see you in back, Maggy?' she asked.

'Of course,' I said, exchanging worried looks with Amy.

Our back office is tiny, the desk sharing space with a refrigerator that held all our dairy products. I settled my butt on the edge of the desk.

'Is everything all right?' I was studying her carefully. 'You look different.'

'I got a haircut at the new place. Dennis of Denmark,' Caron said. 'But this is why I wanted to talk to you.'

She handed me a glossy, oversized sheet of paper. A poster. The headline read: Have you seen this woman?

Below it was a picture of Rachel, probably taken at some party. The missing woman was laughing and care-free in white shorts and a turquoise halter. Ted had been in the photo, too, but in the cropping of the shot, all that remained of him was his left eye, half a nose and mouth on one side of Rachel, and a disembodied hand on the other side.

'Where did you get this?' I asked. The flyers were probably responsible for the media showing up so quickly at Ted and Rachel's house. Whoever was behind them must have called the press as well as getting the posters printed and distributed. Fast work, considering it was only two in the afternoon.

'Eve Slattery stopped by with it,' Caron said.

That would explain it. Eve Whitaker Slattery was Rachel's mother, born into the Whitaker family of Whitaker Foundry fame. Eve's great-grandfather had been the first to realize that Milwaukee was losing its wheat trade to Minneapolis. He shifted to the iron and steel business. There had been gold in them thar' iron ore deposits – figuratively, if not literally, and the Whitakers remained one of Milwaukee's 'First Families' to this day. If Eve Whitaker Slattery wanted something, it happened. And it happened quick.

'Eve Slattery? I didn't know she lives in Brookhills.'

'She doesn't anymore. They're out in lake country now. I knew her through Christ Christian, though, and we've stayed in touch.'

Caron gave me the eye. The one that insinuated that I didn't know as much about our business as I should. 'You do know that we cater Whitaker's breakfast meetings, right?'

The eye always knew. 'Of course,' I said, not quite lying. I did have a vague recollection of delivering gallons of coffee and dozens of doughnuts to a conference room at the Whitaker building just down Civic Drive.

Caron didn't bother drilling me. On the subject of coffee catering, at least. 'You don't seem surprised by the poster. Did you know that Ted's . . .' She hesitated. '. . . wife is missing?'

Caron was uncomfortable calling Rachel 'Ted's wife', because she'd spent most of her adult years calling *me* Ted's wife.

When I met Caron, she was already married to Bernie, who is an attorney. (Yes. Bernie the attorney. *Some*body wasn't thinking when he chose a career.)

Bernie and Ted had been best friends at the University of Wisconsin in Madison. Even though I'd gone there, too, I'd never met either one – probably not a surprise with forty thousand students running around campus. Five years and sixty miles later, Caron had invited me to dinner with her and Bernie and there, sitting on the couch, was Ted. The rest was history. Ancient history.

'Maggy?'

Ted wasn't the only one who got impatient when my train of thought jumped tracks.

'Sorry,' I said automatically. 'Yes, I knew about Rachel. Ted said she didn't come home last night.'

'You talked to Ted?'

'He called this morning.'

'Why in the world would he call *you*?'

I opened my mouth to answer, intending to justify Ted's calling me by using the same reasons that Ted had given me. Thing was, I knew they'd sound lame to Caron. And she'd probably be right.

I shrugged. 'I don't know, honestly. He said he didn't know who else to call.'

'That's lame.'

See?

'You're right,' I said, sliding off the corner of the desk and sinking into the chair next to it. 'But it's Ted.'

'He can be so needy sometimes,' Caron said solemnly.

'I guess.' Which might explain why he 'needed' a brand-new shiny wife. Then he'd gone and misplaced her.

That didn't mean I wasn't worried about her. 'I don't know what to think,' I said. I wasn't sure how much to tell Caron.

I could hear Amy and Sarah, my usual confidante, chatting out in the store. It sounded like Amy was trying to convince Sarah to become vegan and Sarah, who'd never met a processed meat product she didn't like, was sounding interested.

'Have you been to Fresh Foods?' Amy asked. 'They have great organic produce.'

'Yup. In fact, I need to stop there on my way home and get some tofu. Tell Maggy and Caron I said bye, OK?'

The chimes on the door rang and, presumably, Sarah left.

First my cynical friend had gone Brookhills Barbie. Then she'd gone green. And now she'd just . . . gone.

Oh, well, if you can't be with the one you confide in, confide in the one you're with.

I turned to Caron. 'Here's what's going on.'

I laid it all out for her and she listened carefully, one arm propped against the refrigerator. I realized as I talked that I really needed her perspective. Caron had known Ted longer than even I had. She had witnessed all those years of wedded bliss we supposedly had.

'What do you think?' I asked when I was all done. 'Was Rachel right? Do you think Ted was fooling around with other women before Rachel? Or *during* Rachel?'

Caron shook her head, her newly razor-cut hair whirling and then settling obediently back into place. 'I don't know, Maggy. You were living with him and you had no clue. How could I?'

'Because Ted and Bernie were friends. Sometimes friends . . . notice things.' I was hesitating because as we spoke, Caron's face had turned pink. Either it was a reaction to her new hair dye or there was something she wasn't telling me. 'I've known you for too many years, Caron. Give.'

She stood up straight, her face pained. 'It's just that sometimes Ted would call Bernie when it seemed like he should be in meetings or classes or whatever. There were places he mentioned – restaurants, clubs – and this was before he met Rachel.'

I felt like I'd been punched in the stomach. 'So you knew?' I managed.

Caron held up her hands. 'Not knew, Maggy. Never. I'm not even sure that I really even suspected. It's just that in retrospect, it seems . . .'

'Clear,' I supplied. I wasn't feeling sick, so much as I was feeling stupid and humiliated. Stupid that I hadn't seen. And humiliated that others had.

'No, not clear. Possible.' There were tears in Caron's eyes as she came to hug me. 'I'm sorry, Maggy. I wish I had known for sure. I wish I could have warned you.'

I'm not sure I hugged her back, though I should have. It wasn't her fault Ted had cheated on me. Or that I was blind. 'It's Ted,' she said as the bell out front tinkled.

'I know.' I swiped at my nose, which inexplicably had begun to run. 'You didn't do it. I didn't do it. Ted did it. It's Ted, not us.'

Just saying it, I felt stronger.

'No.' Caron pointed at the two-way mirror installed above the desk to give us a view of the store. 'I mean, it's Ted. He just walked in.'

Perfect.

I grabbed a tissue from the box on the desk and blew my nose. Then I stomped out into the store, with Caron on my heels.

Ted was handing Amy a poster, apparently unaware that his mother-in-law had already beaten him to it. 'So if you could just put this up,' he was saying.

I took it out of his hand. 'We'll plaster the place with them, you lying son of a bitch.'

Caron gasped. Amy's eyes widened, but she just stepped back and crossed her arms.

I shook the poster at Ted. 'You were married to me and you screwed her. OK. Maybe those things happen. You *could* have actually fallen in love with her.' I didn't mean to sneer, but I think I did a little.

Ted was looking at me like I'd taken leave of my senses. 'I'm sorry, Maggy, but I did—'

'But she wasn't the first, was she?'

'Believe me, Maggy—'

'Believe you?' I grabbed a tape dispenser from the counter next to the cash register. 'I did believe you, Ted. I believed you when you promised to love, honor and cherish me. I believed you when you said that Eric and I were the best things that ever happened to you.'

Ted was backing up, holding his hands in the air like I had a gun on him.

'I even believed it when you said you loved me.' My voice broke just a little bit there at the end, but I covered by turning on my heel to go to the window, taking the tape with me. I slapped the poster up front and center. Then I turned. 'Just what's your record, Ted? How many of us were you sleeping with at any one time? Three? Four?'

'I'd like to know the answer to that one myself.'

What with the roaring in my ears, I apparently hadn't heard Pavlik come in.

'Sheriff,' Amy said appreciatively. A little *too* appreciatively for my money, but maybe I was just seeing 'other women' everywhere.

Ted's mouth had dropped open while I was berating him. Now he slapped it shut and opened it again. 'What in the world is everyone talking about? I just came here to ask you to help us find Rachel and I walked into –' he pointed vaguely at me, like he didn't know what to call me – 'this.'

I guessed 'this' was as good as anything.

Pavlik looked at me coolly. 'I see you're telling him that his wife knew he was cheating on her.'

That answered the question of what Stephen would tell Pavlik. Everything, from the sounds of it.

Ted was looking back and forth between Pavlik and me. 'Rachel knew what?' Ted asked.

'Not in so many words,' I told Pavlik, 'but—'

Pavlik waved me down. 'Do you suppose you might have clued me in before you told a potential suspect?'

'Potential suspect?' Ted repeated.

At close to six feet tall, Pavlik is a good deal taller than me, but I did my best to get in his face. To my credit, I lowered my voice. 'I did not tell him,' I whispered. '*You* just told him.'

Pavlik's eyes got even darker. I could understand why. I hate doing something stupid, too. Not that it would get me off the hook. 'Are you telling me you weren't about to say something?' he asked.

Fair question. I looked away. 'Not purposely. But I was angry.'

'Join the club,' Pavlik said tersely, his mouth barely moving. 'Let's talk now. Privately.'

He turned to Ted. 'Sit.' He pointed at a chair. Ted sat.

I followed Pavlik into the office. When I stepped in far

enough for the door to be able to swing, he closed the door. Neither of us sat down. I was standing by the refrigerator. Pavlik by the desk.

He went first. 'God damn it, Maggy. Why didn't you tell me you were with Rachel Slattery yesterday afternoon? You were one of the last people who saw her.'

'Are you saying that I'm a suspect?'

'No, but only because according to Stephen Slattery, you were together when his sister left.'

'True. She left at a little after three to go meet an inspector at the Hamilton. Did she keep the appointment?'

Pavlik didn't answer that. Instead, he pulled a notebook and pen out of his coat pocket. 'What time did you leave?'

'Stephen might know exactly what time, because he had a meeting. I think it was about ten after three, though.'

Pavlik nodded, so my recollection must have tallied with what Stephen had told him.

'I'm sorry I didn't tell you about Rachel stopping by,' I said. 'You—'

'Wait.' Pavlik held up his hand. 'She came to see you? Where?'

'My place,' I mumbled.

'Your place? Where you and I were just a few hours ago? Why didn't you mention it?'

'To be fair,' I said, 'we were a little busy. Besides, a visit from your ex-husband's wife isn't exactly pillow talk.'

'And this morning when I got the call?' Pavlik wasn't going to be put off.

'You left so fast that I didn't get a chance.'

'And you don't have a phone? Or you misplaced my number?' He'd down-shifted from 'angry' to 'sarcastic'. Or maybe it was 'sardonic'. Shades of gray, those two.

Since his questions seemed rhetorical, I didn't answer.

Pavlik just glared at me. Then he sat down in the desk chair, flipping his notepad open on the desk in front of him. 'What time?'

'What time did she stop by? A little after noon.' I was glad to have something concrete to offer. 'She asked me for my calendars, which I assume Stephen told you about.'

Pavlik nodded and made a note.

'I wouldn't give them to her outright, but I told her I would go to see Stephen with her. We met at the Slattery Arms at two thirty.'

Pavlik tapped his pen on the pad. 'Did Mrs Thorsen say when she planned to confront her husband with what she knew?'

Calling Rachel 'Mrs Thorsen' seemed designed to hurt me. It worked.

I swallowed. '*Rachel* said she wasn't going to talk to Ted until she had proof. She wanted Stephen to go over the keys and the calendars before her appointment with an attorney on Monday. She wouldn't have said anything until then.'

Pavlik stood up. 'Unless she lost her temper and let it slip.'

'I know I should have called you, but . . .'

'But what?' Pavlik slid the notebook and pen back in his breast pocket.

I weighed sticking with the 'gosh, I didn't have a chance' excuse, versus telling him the deep-down truth. The truth won out. 'I honestly didn't know what I should say. All I had was Rachel's wild accusations and I wanted to—'

As I spoke, I reached up to pick a thread off Pavlik's lapel.

He grabbed my wrist tight and held it. 'Listen to me, Maggy. It's not up to you to decide what I should or shouldn't know. You don't have to protect people from me.'

I pulled my wrist away and rubbed it. 'Really? Because you're so cool and calm you won't go off half-cocked?'

Pavlik shook his head and took a step toward the door. Given the size of the room, that was pretty much all that was necessary. With his hand on the knob, he turned. 'If you can't trust me even in this, even to do my job, how could you trust me in a relationship?'

I opened my mouth to answer, but all the crap I'd been through with Ted came roaring back. Maybe Pavlik was right.

For the second time today, I was too slow to answer a man I cared about.

The sheriff smiled, but it wasn't a happy smile. It wasn't a sad smile either. In fact, I wasn't sure it was a smile at all. 'Goodbye, Maggy.'

He closed the door softly behind him.

Eight

I stayed in the office for a while.
It was quite a long while.

I heard the voices of Ted and Pavlik. The tinkling of the door chimes, just once, and then no more male voices, leading me to believe they'd left together.

Had Pavlik arrested Ted? Or taken him in for questioning?

Frankly my dear, I didn't give a damn. I was too busy licking my wounds and feeling not just a little sorry for myself. I'd told the truth and damned if it *hadn't* set me free, just like they say.

How come when I tried to do the right thing for everyone, I didn't please *any*one, including myself. Especially myself. God, I was a mess.

And I was a lonely mess.

Eric away at school. Ted gone, maybe for twenty to life. Pavlik. I didn't want to think about Pavlik. Even Sarah, my practical, level-headed, obnoxious friend. She'd run off and joined the Barbies. Next thing I knew, she'd be throwing Botox and collagen parties.

I shuddered as there was a knock at the door. 'Are you all right?' Caron called.

I stood up and opened it. 'I forgot about you,' I said.

She got a puzzled look on her face. 'What do you mean?'

'Never mind.' I hugged her. 'Thank you.'

'You're welcome. For whatever I did.' She handed me a towel. 'Do you want a latte? Everyone's gone and I told Amy I could close alone.'

'Sure,' I said, dabbing at my face.

'Are you going to tell me what happened between you

and the sheriff?' Caron asked as she steamed the milk. Whole milk, instead of skim. I was pampering myself.

I grimaced. 'I'm not quite sure myself, but I don't think it was good.'

'No?' As she poured the milk into the mug, she looked up at me, thereby throwing off her aim and sending the milk streaming on to the stainless steel counter.

'No.' I used my crying towel to wipe up the spilled milk. 'He said "goodbye".'

She held out the drink to me. 'Doesn't he usually say goodbye when he leaves?'

'Nobody actually says "goodbye".' I set down the towel and took the latte. 'We say "bye", or "catch you later", or even just "see ya".'

I sank into a chair and took a grateful slurp.

Caron sat down across from me. 'So,' she hazarded, 'if someone actually says "goodbye" . . .?'

'They mean *good*bye. As in bye, for good.' I stood up to snag a raw sugar from the condiment cart.

'Aww, Maggy. I'm so sorry.' Caron sounded like she was going to cry. Didn't I tell you she was a good friend?

I sat back down with the little packet of sugar in my hand. 'Maybe it's for the best,' I said simply, not wanting the conversation to get maudlin. Or more maudlin.

I changed the subject. 'Tell me what happened between Pavlik and Ted while I was in the office.'

Caron's brown eyes got wide. 'I think Pavlik arrested Ted.'

How could Pavlik arrest Ted for a crime he wasn't even sure had been committed? What if Rachel had just run off? Gone on a little vacation?

Caron sometimes heard more than was actually said, if you get my drift. I needed to know Pavlik's precise words.

'What did he say *exactly*?' I asked Caron.

'That he knew that he hadn't killed Rachel.'

Well, that was a relief. But it didn't explain why Caron thought Pavlik had arrested Ted. 'So why do you think he arrested Ted?'

'Because he said he was taking him in for questioning.'

'But why? Hadn't Pavlik just said that Ted hadn't killed Rachel?'

Caron looked puzzled and then her expression cleared. 'Oh, I get it. We're getting our hims crossed.'

'Our "hims"?'

'Actually, I guess it would be our "he's".'

I just looked at her.

'See, it was Ted who said that he, Ted –' she held up her finger – 'knew that *he* – Ted, again – hadn't killed Rachel.'

Ohhh. 'So what did he, *Pavlik . . .*' My God, now I was doing it.

I got hold of myself and started over. 'I mean, what did Pavlik say when Ted said that he –' Caron gave me a look – 'Ted,' I clarified, 'didn't kill Rachel?'

Caron sat back and folded her arms. 'What could he say?'

I was going to scream. 'What *did* he say?'

'He said, "Then how do you know she's dead?"'

I had to admit Pavlik's question was a good one, and I was still thinking about it a half hour later as I cleaned out the pastry cabinet for Caron.

No one had said Rachel was dead. On the other hand, we'd all seen enough episodes of *Law and Order* to assume that when the 'authorities' are questioning you about the disappearance of your wife, they're thinking you 'offed' her. Maybe ninety percent of the time that's not true in real life, but most of us see a whole lot more TV than we do real life.

Which in and of itself is a little sad and a lot scary.

As I brushed the crumbs out of the cabinet, the sleigh bells on the door rang out. I glanced up at the clock. Five minutes to closing. It's what we got for starting on the cleaning early. I heard Caron, who was in the middle of taking apart the espresso machine, swear under her breath.

'Dang it,' a cheery voice said. 'It's not frickin' closing time already, is it?'

Sophie Daystrom, one of my favorite senior citizens, was at the counter. She was wearing a forest green pantsuit – her

Sunday church outfit. You could tell what day of the week it was by what Sophie was wearing. I wondered if she had day-of-the-week undies, too.

'Heck, yes,' I said, standing up and with a broad smile.

There's something about talking to Sophie that makes me break into pseudo-profanity. Maybe it's because every other word out of her mouth was, as Eric would have said at the age of ten, a 'swear'. Sophie is a PG-version of who Sarah will be in thirty or forty years.

'Fudge,' Sophie said, looking wistfully at the pieces of the smoothie machine already laid out on a towel to dry. 'I was hoping for a mango smoothie.'

I held up a basket of muffins. 'Can I tempt you with free pastry, instead?' I asked.

'Free?' Sophie perked right up.

'We either have to throw them away or take them home and I don't think either Caron or I need any more leftover pecan rolls or muffins at home. Right Caron?'

'Right,' Caron said with a sour look. 'Take it all. Again,' she added under her breath.

Either my partner was having another mood swing or there was a story here. Either way, there would be time to talk about it after I foisted all the leftover pastry on Sophie.

'I suppose this is how you keep those girlish figures,' Sophie said as I packed up three blueberry muffins, two pecan rolls, a cinnamon bun and three scones. 'Danged if I shouldn't be doing the same thing now that tennis season is almost here.'

Sophie was eighty, if she was a day, but I heard she played a hell of a game of tennis.

I handed her three white paper bags. 'Just don't eat these all tonight and you'll be fine.'

'Oh, heavens,' she said, waving her veined hand at me. 'I'll put these in the freezer and take one out a day. They'll last me a month.'

'More like a week,' I heard Caron say over the sound of the vacuum that she was now using.

When Sophie had left, I turned on her. 'What was that all about? Did you want that stuff?'

'No way,' Caron said, chasing an errant coffee bean that wouldn't succumb to the vacuum. 'But she shows up at closing time at least a couple of times a week. I know she's doing it to get freebies.'

'Really? I'm surprised.' I slid the coffee bean toward her with the toe of my shoe.

'Why?' Caron took the hose attachment and placed it over the bean. It still wouldn't budge. 'You don't think she'd do that?'

'It's just that I've never noticed.' I leaned down to pick up the bean and tossed it in the waste basket.

Caron flipped the vacuum cleaner off. 'Must be you don't close enough.'

'Must be.' I gave her a smile. 'Hey, thanks for being such a good friend today.'

'You're welcome and I appreciate that you stayed to help me close.' She was rolling up the vacuum cleaner cord. 'I'm going to wash the floor. Will you cut up the boxes?'

'A coffeehouse owner's work is never done,' I said with a feigned sigh. The truth was I was happy to keep busy. I wasn't looking forward to going home and telling Frank about my day.

I spent the next fifteen minutes cutting up cardboard boxes so I could stack the pieces flat and tie them up. When I was finished, I loaded up a grocery cart we kept in the service hall.

Caron stuck her head out into the hallway. 'I'm done. Let me get my purse and the trash and I'll go out to the dumpster with you.'

I balanced one bag of coffee grounds on the back of the cardboard-filled grocery cart and Caron carried another, plus both of our handbags. The service hallway ran behind all of the businesses on our side of the L and let out into the back parking lot where the dumpsters were.

As I rolled the cart up and over the threshold into the parking lot, Caron shivered and looked around.

'Cold?' I asked. It was still near sixty degrees, but maybe her hot flashes had been joined with a few cold ones.

'No, it's just so dark out here it gives me the—'

A metallic clang interrupted her.

'That sounded like it came from the dumpsters,' I whispered.

'Maybe it's a raccoon,' Caron suggested.

'Aren't you the one who said someone's been leaving things? Who do you think is doing it?'

Caron gave me a nervous look. 'You're not going in there are you?'

I eyed the stockade fence that surrounded the dumpsters. A dumpster corral, they called it.

There was just one light in this parking lot, and it did a better job of casting shadows than it did illuminating the corral.

Still, we had a shopping cart of cardboard and trash bags to dispose of, along with Caron's angst about people leaving trash with our garbage. It might seem to be splitting hairs, but I owed it to Caron to solve this problem for her.

'You stay here,' I said. 'I'll go check it out.'

I rolled my cart toward the corral. If there was anyone there, they'd have no doubt, what with the clattering of the cart wheels, that I was coming for a showdown.

'Lock's broken,' I said as I got close enough to see the hasp hanging, the screws that had anchored it pulled from the wood. 'The padlock doesn't do any good if there's nothing to attach it to.'

I lifted the steel plate and dropped it. It made the sound Caron and I had heard. 'I'll have Way get someone to fix it.' Way Benson was our landlord and the owner of Benson Plaza.

I was about to pull the gate open when it swung back at me abruptly. I stumbled against the shopping cart and fell, pulling the shopping cart over on top of me.

As corrugated cardboard cascaded down on me, I heard Caron scream, 'You get away from her, do you hear me?'

Footsteps pounded away. I moved a piece of cardboard from a Chai Tea carton out of the way in time to see a man's figure rounding the corner toward Brookhill Road.

'Are you all right?' Caron asked as she righted the shopping cart.

I shoved the rest of the cardboard away and stood up. 'I am, but who was that?'

'Probably our dumpster dumper,' Caron said. 'We must have caught him in the act.'

She swung open the door. 'Those paint cans weren't here.'

Sure enough, the computer monitors and box spring Caron had told me about had been joined by battered paint cans so old they were red with rust. I hefted one. 'Still full.'

'Full paint cans are against the rules,' Caron wailed. 'And look, he trashed the box spring.'

The fabric on the box spring had been stripped, leaving a network of slats. 'Maybe he was trying to dismantle the thing and put it in the dumpster,' I offered.

'Right, because he's so considerate,' Caron grumbled, slinging her garbage bags into the dumpster.

'Did you get a look at him?' I asked as I trundled the cardboard in from where it lay on the ground outside. 'Is he anybody you recognized?'

'Of course not. If you were going to dump your garbage somewhere, wouldn't you do it as far away as you could?' Caron held the gate for me to go out.

'I suppose.' I looked around the corner at the front parking lot. 'Where's the car?'

'Maybe he parked it where no one would see it,' Caron suggested.

'No, I mean my car,' I said. 'I always . . . damn.'

'What?'

I looked at her. 'I came with Sarah. Can you give me a ride home?'

Happily, Caron could and did. It almost made up for being abandoned by Sarah.

I was bone tired as I unlocked the door to my house. Talk about a full day. A full awful day. Rachel gone, Pavlik dumping me. And it had started out so promising.

I swung open the door, forgetting to give it the Frank Five – that is, to count to five – before I did.

Too late, I heard the pounding of Frank's paws on the polished hardwood floor. Frantically, I tried to pull the door closed, but it was still a good eight inches open when he applied the brakes and careened into the back of the door, thereby catapulting me into the yard on my butt.

What was it with me and doors today?

I got up gingerly and brushed myself off. Then I approached the door again. Listening and hearing nothing, I opened it a crack and peered in. Frank was standing with his head down, regarding the door like a bull about to charge.

'It's OK, Frank,' I called to him. 'I'm here.'

Frank just looked at me. I think. With all that hair, who can tell?

I slipped cautiously through the opening. 'That nasty door can't hurt you now,' I crooned, approaching him. 'Mommy's here.'

Frank looked at me uncertainly. And who can blame him? 'Mommy's here', for God's sake? It was an insult. To both of us.

'I need a glass of wine,' I tried.

Satisfied I was who I claimed to be, Frank relaxed and trotted alongside of me to the kitchen. Now if I could only teach the fuzzy lug how to use a corkscrew, I'd have it made.

Before I had dinner, I needed to check Frank's food bowl – still half full – and clean up the kitchen. I surveyed the remains of the takeout from the night before. What a difference a day makes. A single phone call and everything had changed.

I washed the plates and assorted dishes Pavlik and I had used to reheat the food and dumped the empty boxes in the trash. Then I tied up the bag and looked out the window at the garbage cans, cozied up in the shadows by the side of my garage.

Frank was nosing around the trash bag in my hand. 'Shame on me, Frank,' I said. 'Did I forget to take you out?'

Frank looked at me skeptically. We both knew I'd forgotten to take him out. We also knew I had an ulterior motive.

'Fine,' I admitted. 'I'd like your company. A garbage bogey man knocked me down and even though I know he didn't follow me home, I'm a little nervous.'

If I could have seen Frank's eyes, I'm certain he would have been rolling them. Nonetheless, he padded to the back door. I opened it and he headed for the nearest tree. I went for the garbage cans.

It was hard to be nervous with a hundred pounds of sheepdog watering a tree nearby. Putting the metal top back on the can, I waited for Frank to finish and then called him. Time for dinner.

I'd been trying to cut back on wine, not only because of the alcohol, but the empty calories. Tonight, though, empty calories were on the menu. I even dug out my secret stash of organic chocolate. Dark chocolate with crushed hazelnut brittle in it. Heaven. I pulled out a plate and put the candy bar on it. Then I added some pretzels. Wine, chocolate and salty snacks. The triumvirate.

But I still needed the wine. I opened the fridge to see if I had a partial bottle.

I did, of course. The bottle of red Zinfandel that I had opened when Rachel was there. Just yesterday, but it seemed like a lifetime ago.

'I hope it isn't Rachel's lifetime ago,' I said as I reached in the cupboard for a wine glass.

Frank looked at me. Perhaps it was because I keep the doggy treats next to the wine glasses. I liked to think, though, that he was listening to me. Just in case, I slipped him a bone-shaped treat.

'So what do you think, Frank?' I asked as I poured myself a glass of Zin. 'Do you think Rachel is OK?'

Frank was too busy wolfing down the treat to answer. He did wiggle his butt, which was the equivalent of a wag, given that he really didn't have much of a tail.

I added a couple of doggy treats to my plate and took it and my glass into the living room.

'And if she's not OK,' I continued, settling down on the couch, 'did Ted have anything to do with it?'

I was thinking about Ted's reaction to Pavlik's appearance at the store today. He – that would be *Ted* – looked shocked when Pavlik told him Rachel knew he was cheating on her.

'So was he honestly surprised?' I asked Frank, holding up another treat to get his attention. 'Or is he just a good actor?'

Frank answered by nearly taking off my fingers, going after the bone. I didn't need his opinion, though. The fact that Ted had fooled me for so long told me he was a good liar. What it didn't tell me was whether he was lying this time.

I felt like I was going around in circles. Looking for answers to questions that hadn't even been asked yet. First and foremost, was Rachel dead? Because if she wasn't dead, if she was just fine, maybe sitting on a beach or having a facial, I was going to kill her.

I looked at Frank, like he'd heard my thoughts. 'Not literally, you understand.'

Frank gave me a disdainful look and went to lie down by the cold fireplace.

I'd had problems dealing with males of both species today. Ted I'd played Jekyll and Hyde with, running to his rescue this morning and then reaming him out this afternoon. Pavlik, I'd made love with and then . . .

'Pavlik left me,' I said, and even to my ears it sounded plaintive. Whiny, even.

Left me? How could he leave me when he'd never been with me. Except for that once. Once and once only. Last night. And again this morning. OK, twice and twice only.

'He says I don't trust him.'

Frank gave me the eye.

'Maybe he's right,' I said. 'I like to make my own decisions. Is that a crime?'

Frank got up and stalked out.

'At least *I* never disappoint me,' I yelled after him.

Then I drained my wine glass and went to bed.

Nine

I was busy trying to find the store keys in my bag or I would have seen him.

Uncommon Grounds opens at six thirty in the morning, so that means the person opening has to be there at five thirty to plug in the brewers, grind the coffee and follow the rest of the seventeen-step A.M. Checklist I'd put together when we opened.

Sadly, this morning I was the one opening the store, which meant that I was reduced to following my own rules. I hated that.

Since it was the middle of April, it was dark at five thirty. Hell, it's nearly always dark at five thirty. And when it's not, it should be.

It was tough to be cheery at this time of the morning. You had to talk yourself into it. Remind yourself that the days were getting longer and that by this time next month, maybe the sun *would* be coming up when you opened. Or think about all the things you would do this afternoon, because you'd gotten work out of the way early.

I was in the midst of my atta-girl-Maggy morning pep talk, when I pulled into the parking lot. The tall lights meant to illuminate the lot were flickering, apparently sensing the approaching sunrise. There was no other evidence of it, though, as I got out of the car. The lot was shadowy, with no lights coming from the storefronts on either side of Uncommon Grounds.

As I said, I was getting the store keys out of my bag as I approached the door.

A figure stepped out of the darker shadows into the lighter ones. 'Maggy!'

In a romance, it would be Pavlik, who, unable to sleep, had come to the store to apologize. In a slasher movie, it would have been the bogey garbage man come to waste me.

But this wasn't a romance or a slasher pic. It was my life.

'Ted?'

What I could see of him looked like at least part of my scenario was true. He hadn't slept. I felt a pang of sympathy, misplaced though it might be.

'You scared me,' I said, trying to fit the key into the lock by touch. 'What are you doing here?'

I pushed open the door and picked my way through the tables and chairs to the wall next to the bean bins, where the light switches are. I normally would turn on just the back lights, so passers-by wouldn't think we were open and stop by before I had the coffee ready. Given the lurker last night as well as Ted's unexpected appearance, I figured flipping on all the lights was warranted.

My ex-husband still hadn't said anything beyond my name. I turned to survey him. Sure enough, he had on the clothes he'd been wearing yesterday.

'Did you escape from jail?'

The old Ted would have rolled his eyes. Maybe even given me a little sneer.

The new unimproved Ted, though, collapsed in a chair, elbows propped on the table in front of him, head in his hands.

'Oh, my God, you did!' I gasped.

This time I got the eye-roll, thank the Lord.

'I wasn't arrested,' he said. 'The sheriff just wanted to ask some questions.' He peered at me from between his fingers. 'I don't get what you see in that guy.'

'Me, neither.' I sat down opposite him. 'So did Pavlik question you all night?'

Ted gave me a surprised look. 'No, of course not. An hour or two maybe. Why would you think that? Do you know something?'

'Believe me,' I said, 'I am the last person Pavlik is going to tell anything from now on. No, I asked because you look like you haven't slept. You're also wearing the same clothes you had on yesterday.'

Ted looked down at his blue golf shirt and khaki pants. 'No, I'm not.' He sounded offended at the idea.

'You had on khaki pants and a blue golf shirt,' I said.

'I have eight pairs of khakis and seventeen golf shirts. And this shirt is navy. Yesterday's was royal.'

Navy versus royal? 'Geez, when did you get to be such a girl?'

'Rachel said I needed to upgrade my wardrobe,' Ted said, flushing. 'She said she wouldn't put up with my running around looking like a slob anymore.'

'You've worn khakis and golf shirts ever since I've known you,' I pointed out. 'Now you just know what colors they are.'

'And I don't wear cargos anymore,' Ted said, standing up to show me his flat-front pants. 'Or pleated fronts. Rachel says no man should wear pleats.'

'Except Sean Connery.' But then that man could be ninety years old and in a wheelchair, and I'd still go to bed with him.

'That's a kilt,' Ted said sourly. He was aware of my obsession with Sean.

'Yes, it is,' I said dreamily. Then I stood up. 'You should call Eric this morning.'

Ted took a deep breath and let it out slowly. 'I don't want to involve him in this.'

'I don't either, but it will be worse if he hears it on the news.'

Ted bowed his head.

'Listen, if you want to hang around, we can call him together,' I offered. 'First, though, I have to get through my checklist.'

'What checklist?' Ted seemed eager to contemplate anything but waking our son to tell him that his stepmother was missing and his father was being questioned by the police.

I opened the cabinet door over the sink and pulled a list off the inside of the door, where it was taped and safely protected in plastic.

I handed it to him, figuring it would keep him busy. 'This checklist.'

Ted took it.

A.M. Checklist
- ☐ Turn on backlights
- ☐ Plug in and turn on coffee brewers (need 15 minutes to heat)
- ☐ Turn on digital coffee scale
- ☐ Grind coffee for brewed coffees of the day (one regular and one decaf – see schedule) on regular grind
- ☐ Grind decaf French Roast for espresso (fine)
- ☐ Cone grinder filled? Grind first lot
- ☐ Run blinds for espresso
- ☐ Run plain water through both brewers
- ☐ Post names of brewed coffees (better to do the night before)
- ☐ Fill bud vases and put on tables
- ☐ Fill creamer and put on condiment cart
- ☐ Brew coffees of the day
- ☐ Fill baskets in bakery case
- ☐ Put cash in cash register
- ☐ Bring in newspaper (should arrive around 06:15)
- ☐ Turn on front lights, music, flip sign and unlock door at 06:30

'I guess I'm glad you didn't run our household like a business.'

'If I had,' I said, plugging in the brewers and flipping on the scale, 'you would have known exactly how many shirts you had and what colors they were.'

'Rachel doesn't treat me like a business. Besides, she's missing,' Ted said sternly. 'Could you cut her some slack?'

He was right. 'Did Pavlik say if they knew anything more?'

'If they do, he's not telling me any more than he's telling you.' Ted sounded like a sad puppy. 'He says Rachel thought I was cheating on her.'

'Weren't you?' I didn't trust myself to look at him, just continued shoveling coffee beans into the cone grinder.

'Of course not. I loved Rachel.'

'I've heard that before,' I mumbled, flipping on the grinder.

'What?' Ted yelled over the din.

'I said –' turning back to him – 'that you supposedly loved me, too, but you didn't have any trouble cheating on me.'

'That was different.' He stood up and rounded the counter to where I was.

'Different? What was different about it? You were married to me and you said you loved me, but you had an affair with a younger woman. You are married to Rachel and you say you love her. Now she says you had an affair. What happened, Ted? Did you meet somebody younger again? What are you down to now? Twelve-year-olds?'

'Why would I be interested in adolescents?' He took a step toward me. 'After all, I was married to one for nearly twenty years.'

Low blow. Though not completely without truth.

I brandished the coffee scooper at him. 'Very funny. But the fact is that you slipped up. You were caught with someone – someone that Rachel thinks you were seeing when you and I were still married.'

Ted stopped dead. 'She does?'

'She does.' I flipped off the grinder, which had run out of beans to grind. 'Is she right?'

'Who?' Ted sputtered. 'And where and when?'

Now if we only had 'what' and 'why', we'd have it covered. 'I don't know where or when, but I think the "who" is Emma.'

'Emma Byrne?'

Yeah, like there were more beautiful raven-haired, blue-eyed Emmas that Ted had known since dental school. 'Yes, Emma Byrne.'

'But Rachel knows Emma,' Ted protested. 'She used to work for her.'

'And I knew Rachel,' I said, crossing my arms. 'She

worked for *you*. It not only didn't stop you, but it was great cover. Just friends, right?'

If Ted was having an affair with Emma, it might have been going on for years. Maybe even dating back before we were married. She could be his Camilla Parker Bowles to my Princess Diana.

'Is it all a lie?' I asked Ted, a little dazed.

He'd been saying something I hadn't heard. He stopped. 'What's a lie?'

'Our story.'

'I don't understand.' He was looking at me like I was crazy.

'You know, the story of "us". The one I tell myself about you and me. How we met. How we fell in love. Buying the house. Having Eric.'

I moved closer to Ted. 'I'd managed to salvage part of that. I honestly thought we had some good years.'

'A lot of good years,' Ted said softly.

As I looked up at him, the door tinkled.

'We're not open yet,' I said, stepping away from Ted. I wasn't sure if I should be grateful for the interruption or irritated by it. 'I don't have the coffee brew—'

'Apparently you're open for *some* people.'

This time, the visitor *was* Pavlik. But he sure didn't look romantic. Instead, he looked official.

I tried to put the best face on it that I could. 'Much as I love the fact that people seem to gravitate here,' I said, 'I'd prefer that both of you do it during business hours.'

'These are my business hours,' Pavlik said. 'I know why I'm here. Why is he?' He gestured to Ted.

'I couldn't sleep,' Ted said.

'So you come here?'

'His mom is in Paris,' I explained.

'Berlin. Or London,' Pavlik said dryly. 'You already tried that one.'

'It's true,' I said. 'I mean, except for the city. The woman gets around.'

'As does her son. How come when I go looking for Thorsen, all I have to do is figure out where you are?'

Good question. I looked at Ted. 'Why is that?'

'I'm not sure. I guess I just needed—'

Pavlik interrupted. 'What you "need" right now is a lawyer.' He signaled and two uniformed sheriff's deputies stepped in. As they approached, Pavlik turned back to Ted.

'Rachel Slattery Thorsen's body was found in Lake Michigan an hour ago. Tor Thorsen, you have the right to remain . . .'

I don't remember the rest of the rights Pavlik read to Ted. What I do remember vividly was the look on Ted's face. Shocked. Frightened.

And totally alone.

I wasn't sure what to do. I couldn't leave the store, but should I call a lawyer for Ted? It really wasn't my place any longer, but my ex-husband had looked so shell-shocked as Pavlik took him off, that he might not be capable of doing it himself.

Not that I was any better equipped. I didn't know any lawyers besides my divorce attorney and Bernie, who did corporate work. I didn't think either of them would be much help getting Ted out of the slammer.

Having no answers, I did the only thing I knew how to do. I tackled the checklist at hyper-speed. By the time Caron arrived at six thirty, I was filling the cash register. She had the newspaper in her hand and dropped it on the reading counter next to the condiment cart.

'Good morning,' she said cheerily, picking up the list Ted had left on the table. 'Do you still need this after all this time?' she asked, waving it at me.

'Believe me, I know all seventeen steps by heart.'

'There are sixteen,' she said, hanging it back up.

'Are not,' I said. Focusing on minutia was a whole lot easier than focusing on the larger issues. Things like Rachel being dead. Or Ted being arrested for her murder.

'There are sixteen steps on your list, not seventeen. By the way, did the bakery deliver the cookies in the shape of apples? People have been asking for them for teacher appreciation.'

'No, I mean, yes. They're there.' I pointed at a white

pastry box. 'I've been calling it the seventeen-step checklist for a year now. Why haven't you corrected me?'

She shrugged. 'It didn't seem important.' She picked up her Uncommon Grounds apron and slipped it over her head, tying it around her waist. 'So are you feeling any better? What's new?'

What's new? Let's see . . .

'Ted was at the door when I got here this morning. Then Pavlik arrived, really angry to find Ted here.'

'Angrier than yesterday?' Caron asked.

'Oh, yeah.'

'What did he say?'

'He said that Rachel's body was found in Lake Michigan and he read Ted his rights.'

Caron had gone white. 'Are you kidding?'

'I have a weird sense of humor, but not that weird. Do you think Bernie could recommend a lawyer if Ted needs one?'

Caron scrunched up her nose. 'I don't know if Bernie knows any defense attorneys, but I can ask him. Did Pavlik say how she died?'

Good question. 'I didn't even think to ask.'

She poured me a cup of coffee and handed it to me. 'That's because you're in shock like I was when I found Patricia's body last year. Your mind doesn't work straight.'

I wished I'd been as understanding when she'd gone brain dead on me back then. It probably would have been a lot more effective than the passive-aggressive approach I'd taken with her.

'Think it's in the paper?' Caron unfolded the newspaper she'd placed on the reading stand.

'I don't see how it could be. Pavlik said they found Rachel about an hour ago. The paper's deadline is eleven p.m.'

That, at least, was good news. I needed to call Eric and tell him what had happened to Rachel, but I would almost certainly get his voicemail this early in the morning. I preferred not to leave a message or wake him up to tell him the news, but I also didn't want him to see it in the morning paper. Not that Eric read news from anything but a computer screen. And that was usually accidental as he was logging on to e-mail.

Besides, Eric was in Minneapolis/St. Paul – the Twin Cities, or just the Cities to people up there. The Cities were five hours away from Milwaukee and served by different newspapers and television stations.

Still, judging by the news trucks at Ted and Rachel's house yesterday, the discovery of Rachel's body could well make the national news today. Especially given the Slattery and Whitaker family connections.

What to do, what to do.

'We don't have a television here,' Caron said, as if she were reading my mind, 'so we can't even see if it's on the news. Do we know who found the body or where?'

'We know nothing,' I said, 'because I asked nothing. Not that Pavlik would have told me, the mood he was in.'

'There is that.' Caron had poured a cup of coffee for herself and now she took a sip. Finding it too hot, she blew on it and set it down. 'So the body was found an hour before the sheriff came here at, what? Six?'

'Maybe quarter to,' I said.

'Then that means somebody was near the lake at four thirty or five.'

'An early-morning boater, maybe?' I suggested. 'The weather's been really nice.'

'Or maybe a fisherman or jogger.'

'Which means the body was probably inside the break-water.' My brain was starting to function again. 'Maybe near the park or the marina. Someplace downtown, at least.'

'Probably,' Caron agreed. 'I'm surprised they were able to identify her so quickly.'

'She was only missing for a day,' I said. 'So she couldn't have been in the water long.'

I was thinking about the last time I had seen Rachel. The boots. The miniskirt. 'I wonder if she was still wearing what she had on when she came by my house on Saturday.'

'She'd have to have been, right? Ted says she never came home.' Caron looked at me.

I looked at Caron.

'You do believe him, right?' she asked.

'Of course. Why would he lie?'

'Why would he?' she echoed.

Only if he'd killed her and dumped her body in the lake.

Ten

Who needs a television when you have customers eager to bring you all the news that's fit to repeat?

First up to the cash register was Laurel Birmingham, Brookhills town clerk. Laurel is a tall, well-endowed redhead, who delights in wearing low-cut tops. Her breasts had seemed especially perky since she came back from vacation. I suspected a boob job or a really good sale at Victoria's Secret.

'Did you hear?' she asked breathlessly.

Most of the time Laurel was first with the news, so her face dropped when I said I knew Rachel's body had been found. Almost immediately, I realized my mistake.

'But how could you have seen the news?' Laurel asked. 'Haven't you been here since . . .' A knowing look. 'Ohhh, your sheriff.'

I did a quick mental tally. I could tell her the truth, but it would raise the question of why Ted was here at Uncommon Grounds in the first place. That, in itself, would inspire all sorts of gossip. Since people were already queuing up behind Laurel, I thought the simplest answer was the best.

'Yes,' I said, with what I hoped was a demure smile. 'Pavlik told me.'

It was true. He'd told me as he led Ted off.

'The sheriff arrested him here,' Caron said from behind me.

I turned and gave her a look that should have turned her into salt.

She waved me away. 'It's impossible to keep secrets from Laurel. You might as well come clean.'

'She's right, you know.' Laurel signaled that she wanted her usual. 'It'll be in the sheriff's report anyway.'

Damn public records. 'We don't know that he was arrested. He simply went with the sheriff's deputies.'

'Holy crap!' a voice exclaimed from the back of the line. 'Did they read him his rights?'

Sophie.

Henry Wested, who lives at the assisted living facility on Poplar Creek, was standing next to her.

'Even if they did,' he said to her, 'it doesn't mean the man has been arrested, only that he was taken into custody for questioning.'

Henry was looking natty in his customary gray fedora, a little red feather in the brim. Sophie was wearing her Monday outfit – red pants and a black top with red cherries artfully scattered. They made a cute couple and I had my suspicions they actually *were* a couple.

'They didn't read me *my* rights,' a man half-hidden behind Laurel said. 'But then maybe I'm not a suspect.'

At the sound of his voice, Caron's face went beet red. That alone would have been enough to tell me who the mystery man was, even if I hadn't recognized the voice.

'Roger Karsten, as I live and breathe,' Sophie said. 'What the heck are you doing back in Brookhills?'

Caron slid Laurel's large decaf with steamed milk across the counter to her and slipped behind me. Roger was Brookhills' former building inspector and he and Caron had a . . . history.

'I'm working in Milwaukee.' Roger flashed Caron a toothy grin by way of me. 'I have my own company now.'

Probably Gigolos R Us.

Roger stepped up to the counter and handed me a card that read 'Karsten Building Inspections, Inc.'

'So you're the inspector Rachel was meeting at the Hamilton?' I asked. I might not like Roger, but I was willing to set that aside long enough to pump him for information.

'Was supposed to meet,' he corrected, giving a swipe to his slightly too long and slightly too sun-bleached hair. 'She never showed.'

'Are you sure?' Laurel asked. The whole crowd was paying rapt attention.

For his part, Roger seemed equally mesmerized by Laurel's cleavage. 'Positive,' he said, not looking up from her breasts. 'I . . . um, waited until three forty-five.' He licked his lips.

Ugh. 'All of fifteen minutes?' I demanded.

'That's ten minutes longer than he waited when he worked for the town,' someone said. 'Must be all that money the Slatterys have.'

We all turned toward the newcomer and a couple of people gasped.

'You're wearing a tennis skirt,' Laurel said to Sarah.

Old news. What I was amazed at, though, was the time. To my knowledge, Sarah had never seen a sunrise. 'You're looking awfully bright-eyed and bushy-tailed for six forty-five in the morning.'

But Laurel was studying Sarah's face. 'Are you wearing make-up?'

Sarah stalked past her and up to the counter, edging Roger aside. 'No.'

'You are, too,' Laurel insisted. 'You have mascara on.'

'I just have dark lashes.' Sarah batted her eyes. 'Besides, look who's talking. Your boob is falling out.'

'Damn. It's this sweater,' Laurel tucked the miscreant back in as Roger watched appreciatively. 'Sometimes my breasts escape.'

'The size of those honkers these days, she better put out an APB,' Sarah said under her breath as Roger moved closer to Laurel.

I giggled. I don't normally giggle, so I could only put my recent rash down to stress.

'Who are you playing tennis with?' I asked Sarah as Roger and Laurel moved away. I was hoping it was Emma Byrne. I was also hoping they were meeting here at Uncommon Grounds. It certainly seemed like everyone else was.

'Emma. She's meeting me here.'

Bingo.

As if by magic, the door opened again and in walked Emma Byrne tucked into a white tennis outfit. Roger's head swiveled.

'Morning,' Emma said, catching sight of us.

I didn't know how to broach the subject gracefully, and besides, I didn't want to be tactful. I wanted to drop a bombshell and see what happened.

I beckoned her over. 'Did you hear? Rachel Thorsen's body was found in Lake Michigan this morning.'

Sarah's mouth dropped open. Caron, aka Miss Manners, smacked me one.

Emma, however, seemed about to pass out. She went pale and her eyes widened so much I could see white all the way around the blue iris.

Dropping her tennis bag, she put her hand to her mouth. 'How . . .?' She cleared her throat. 'Does Ted know?'

'Ted was arrested,' Laurel said, moving away from Roger. 'He was arrested right here in the store not an hour ago. Right, Maggy?'

'Is that true?' Emma asked me. 'Has Ted been arrested?'

'All I know is that he was here waiting for me when I opened,' I said, watching for her reaction. Getting none, I added, 'The sheriff arrived, told us what happened and Ted left with him.'

'They took him into custody for questioning,' Sophie said, beaming proudly at Henry, the source of her knowledge. 'That's why they had to read him his rights.'

'They read him his rights?' Emma asked. 'But do they think . . . do they know how she died?'

Apparently everyone thought to ask that question except me.

'There weren't any specifics on the news,' Laurel said, 'only that an unidentified woman's body was found by the rocks on the breakwater.'

I looked at her. 'Unidentified?'

Laurel shrugged. 'I only had a chance to say "Did you hear?" before you jumped in. You're the one who told me they took Ted away. It doesn't take a genius to put two and two together and figure out it was Rachel.'

I'd been scammed. 'Listen, if they haven't publicly identified the body yet, maybe they want it kept quiet.'

Laurel tish-toshed me. 'If the sheriff is questioning Ted,

they know it's Rachel. They're probably just waiting until it's confirmed with dental records or DNA or whatever before releasing it to the press.'

Both of which they could find in plentiful measure at Ted's office or house.

Emma must have been thinking the same thing. She snagged her bag. 'Sarah, forgive me, but Ted and I have been friends for a long time. I'd like to see what I can do to help.'

'Not a problem,' Sarah called to Emma's back as it went out the door.

Then she said to me, 'The other woman, I presume?'

'I think to me, she'd be the *other*, other woman.' I turned to Caron, who had been trying to wait on customers throughout all this.

'I really think I should call Eric before this gets out,' I told her apologetically. 'Can you hold down the fort for a couple minutes?'

Sarah shrugged her bag off her shoulder and raised her hand. 'I can help.'

'That's fine,' Caron said gratefully, looking at the growing line. 'You pour coffee and handle bakery and I'll do the specialty drinks.'

'She likes to keep you away from the frothing wand,' I told Sarah, putting my hand on her arm. 'Thank you.'

'That's not what Eric is going to say when you wake him up before seven,' Sarah said, tying on an apron.

'Don't I know it,' I muttered. 'Especially with news like this.'

Once in the office, I closed the door and sat down at the desk. I'd wanted to call Eric when I knew he'd be up, but I also didn't want to chance missing him. Digging through my purse, I pulled out my cellphone and punched in his number.

As I suspected it would, my call went to voicemail. I'd try texting. Where Eric would ignore calls, he never received a text message he wouldn't answer. Or at least read.

Eric sent a thousand text messages a month, the reason we had 'free texting' on our phones. When I'd asked how he managed to fit both texting and school into his day, he'd looked at me like I was crazy. 'Texting is fast.'

'It is not,' I protested. 'It takes me ten minutes to write a message.'

In self-defense – so I wouldn't cut off his cellphone – Eric taught me how to write text messages using something called predictive text or T9. Until then, I'd been punching in single letters – pushing the '(2)abc' key on the cellphone once for 'a', twice for 'b', three times for 'c'. It took forever.

With T9, though, you tap each key once and a computer built into your phone predicts the word you're typing by the combination of keys you've pushed. Push '(8)tuv', '(4)ghi' and '(3)def' and the computer knows you want the word 'the'.

Miraculous. And, OK, maybe it *still* takes a lot longer than actually calling someone, but at least I could count on getting Eric's attention, even if he was half asleep.

I texted, 'Call me.'

Like I said, miraculous, but not necessarily infallible. 'Me' came up as 'of', but I fixed it with a push of a button and sent it off.

And waited.

I was about to give up and go up front to help, when the familiar beep-beep-beep alerted me to a text message.

'Asleep,' it said.

I punched in his phone number and hit send. He answered, after a fashion, on the third ring. 'Huh?'

'Hi, sweetie,' I said.

A groan on the other end.

'Listen, I'm sorry to wake you up.'

This time a sigh, followed by the pounding of a pillow and then, finally, a barely discernible: 'Class is noon.'

Honest to God, Eric was starting to *sound* like a text message. No hellos, no goodbyes, and no prepositions.

'Eric,' I said, 'I have bad news.'

'What?' I could hear him sit up, suddenly alert. 'Are you all right?'

'I'm fine,' I started. 'It's—'

'Grandma or Grandpa? Or Grandma Thorsen?' Then I

heard real fear creep into his voice. 'Or Dad? Is Dad OK?'

I struggled to control my own voice and not show any fear for Ted. First things, first. 'It's Rachel, Eric. She's dead. She—'

'Rachel?'

I could hear the disbelief in his voice. Rachel was young. Not all that far from his age. Young people didn't die.

'How?' Eric sounded hollow.

'I don't know. They found her body in Lake Michigan this morning. I didn't want you to hear it on the news.'

'Why are you calling instead of Dad?' he asked. 'Is he OK?'

We didn't raise a dumb kid.

'Dad is fine, but he's been worried. He's at the police station now.' It was true as far as it went.

'Did she jump?' Eric asked. 'Why would she do that?'

'Nobody knows what happened at this point. When I do find out more, though, I'll call you.'

'Will you have Dad call me when he can?' Eric asked. 'He might need to talk to someone.'

The remark was so quintessentially Eric that I wanted to cry. 'I will,' I promised. Then I told him that I loved him and hung up.

A knock at the door. 'We've whittled the line down and I have to leave. Did you get hold of the kid?' Sarah asked.

'I did.' I stuffed my cell back in my purse and my purse back in the desk drawer. 'He wants Ted to call, because Eric figures Ted probably needs someone to talk to.'

'You and Ted did good with him.' Sarah hung up her apron.

'I didn't tell him his father was being questioned by the police.'

Sarah shrugged. 'Why would you? It won't help Ted and it sure won't help Eric.'

'I know, but I don't like keeping things from him.'

'With luck, maybe there won't be anything to tell him,' Sarah said.

'And if Ted is arrested?' I asked, following her out into the store.

'*Then* you'll tell him.' She picked up her tennis bag and left.

I didn't have much time to think about what I should or shouldn't have told Eric as Caron and I dealt with the second morning rush – commuters picking up their coffee on the way to work in downtown Milwaukee.

For years, I'd made the trek myself, so I was sympathetic to people needing to get their coffee and be on their way. To make it easier for them, I'd set up an express lane for customers who wanted plain old brewed coffee. That way, they didn't have to wait behind a 'decaf triple-shot, skim, sugar-free vanilla latte' person. Believe me, it was healthier for everyone.

I worked the express lane today, both because Caron prefers to chat with people as she makes their specialty drinks and . . . I don't. Especially today.

Not that I couldn't hear the discussion, which naturally centered on the discovery of 'the body'. Happily, between pouring coffee and brewing a fresh pot every five minutes, I couldn't very well be expected to join in.

Besides, everyone knew I was Ted's ex-wife and would be sensitive to my feelings, right?

'I understand your ex-husband was taken into custody right in front of you,' a voice said. 'How did that make you feel?'

I looked up to see Kate McNamara, editor of *The Observer*, Brookhills weekly newspaper. In addition to editing *The Observer*, Kate is staff photographer and has been known to sell the occasional ad. She also reads the school lunch menu on the local cable access station.

I would wonder how she found the time, if I didn't know that most of the news she ran in *The Observer* was lifted directly from the daily newspaper, the *CitySentinel*.

Kate McNamara is, simply put, a pain in the butt. 'The latte line is over there, Kate,' I told her.

'It's Kat. And I'll have a black coffee today.'

'Kat? You're changing your name?'

She sniffed. 'I didn't change my name, I shortened it. I'm entitled.'

'Don't you think Kat is a little trendy?' I reached for a fresh pot of coffee, proud of the restraint I'd shown by not adding, 'for a woman your age'.

'I think it says who I am.' She pulled her notebook out of her over-stuffed bag. 'Quick. Cunning.'

And totally self-absorbed. She was right. It was the perfect name for her.

'Now tell me,' she continued. 'What do you know about your husband killing his new wife?'

I put the pot I had in my hand back on the burner and picked up the one I'd been about to dump down the sink. 'Nothing.' I poured the old coffee into a road cup and handed it to her.

'Come on, Maggy. You were married to the man for twenty years. Can you honestly tell me you don't know if he killed his wife?'

Actually, I honestly *could* tell her that. But I wouldn't. 'I am not going to talk to you about this, Kate.'

'Kat,' she corrected.

'Kate.'

'Kat.'

'Children.' Caron stepped between us with a half-made cappuccino in her hand. 'Call each other names . . .'

'Nicknames,' I corrected.

'. . . later,' Caron finished, glaring at me. 'Please. We have customers.'

Caron was right. And all of them were staring at us.

I turned to Kate/Kat. 'Listen to me,' I hissed in a low whisper, 'this is personal. I am not going to give you a quote. So, please, go away.'

Kate just looked at me.

'Please go away, *Kat*.'

She put up her hands. 'Fine,' she said loudly enough that people could hear. 'I have no intention of intruding on your grief. If there's anything that you would like to say to the public, though, I hope you'll call me.'

She pulled a card out of her bag and slid it across the counter, and then she was gone.

*   *   *

'Kat McNamara, Investigative Reporter on the Prowl?' Caron said, picking up the card a couple of hours later.

'I hope Kat chokes on a hairball,' I muttered.

I was busy wiping down the tables for the next rush of the day, which would be the tennis moms. Unlike the soccer moms, whose kids played soccer, tennis moms were simply moms who played tennis. So, technically, you could be both a tennis mom and a soccer mom. And most probably were. Sports were big in Brookhills.

The tennis moms would have had just enough time to get the kids off to school and themselves off to a couple of sets of tennis before coming by for coffee. The weird thing was that despite playing tennis, none of them seemed to sweat. Stepford Moms.

Moms.

I sat down in the chair I'd been wiping off.

'You OK?' Caron asked.

'Yeah. It just hit me again that Rachel was pregnant. Two lives lost.'

'How far along was she?' Caron asked.

'I don't know, but it had to be pretty early in the pregnancy. She certainly wasn't showing.'

'Do you think the police know?'

'Pavlik is the one who told me,' I said.

Caron took the rag out of my hand and continued cleaning the tables. 'You know, I was thinking that you should go see the sheriff. Maybe you can find out what's happening with Ted and patch things up with Pavlik at the same time.'

'That's not a bad idea.' Not the 'patching things up', because it probably wouldn't be that easy, but I really did want to check up on Ted. If I didn't owe it to Ted, I did to our son.

Besides, why should Emma Byrne have all the fun?

When I finished work at two o'clock, I drove home, showered and changed. Then I dialed Pavlik's cellphone number. He didn't answer.

'He has to have his cellphone,' I said to Frank. 'He's the sheriff.'

Unless 'the sheriff' was avoiding my calls.

I hung up the phone and pulled out my keys. I'd go to his office and drop in unannounced. How bad could it be?

I had no idea.

Pavlik was in his office.

'Can I come in?' I asked, sticking my head around the doorjamb.

'Certainly.' It was what you said to a stranger. Or, even worse, a constituent. The sheriff waved me to a chair next to his desk. I closed the door and went to sit. The chair made a whistley noise.

'First, I want to apologize,' I started.

'No apology necessary,' he said.

That was it. That's all he said. His eyes were neutral. Not blue. Not stormy gray. Not anything.

Feeling awkward, I glanced down at his desk. 'Those are my calendars.'

'I know.'

I was getting a little tired of the polite little responses. 'Don't you need my permission to have them?'

'They're evidence. Stephen Slattery turned them over to me.'

Two sentences. I was making progress. I was also feeling uncomfortable about Pavlik pawing through my calendars. Since he'd already pawed *me*, though, I wasn't sure why. 'Am I going to get them back?'

'Eventually.'

Back to single word responses. 'Aren't you being a bit juvenile?'

Pavlik's eyes darkened, just a little. It felt like progress. 'I'm being professional, Maggy. I don't know what else I can be with you.'

I wasn't sure what to say to that. 'Are you still holding Ted?'

His eyes went even darker. 'For now.'

I stood up. 'Does he need a lawyer?'

'If he wants one.'

I wondered if Emma had been there. The way things

were going between Pavlik and me, she'd probably be more help to Ted than I could be. 'Did you see a woman? Black hair, blue eyes?'

'Can't say. Why?' Pavlik looked suddenly interested.

'She's a lawyer Ted knows,' I fibbed. I had no intention of telling Pavlik that I suspected that the blue-eyed brunette was Ted's affairee. If that were a word. I wasn't sure why I was trying to protect Ted, beyond the fact Pavlik was being an ass.

As I turned to leave, I caught sight of a stack of key cards next to Pavlik's computer. 'What are those?'

'You know what,' Pavlik said. 'They're your ex-husband's key cards.'

I hadn't literally meant 'what are those'. I wanted to know where Pavlik had gotten them. Had Rachel found more than what she'd left with Stephen?

'Did Stephen give them to you?' I asked.

Pavlik looked at me quizzically. 'No, these were found in the victim's purse. Why?'

Before I could answer the office door flew open.

The woman standing in the doorway looked just like her pictures on the society page. Petite, with upswept blonde hair. She was wearing a white wool suit and looked very chic. And very angry.

Despite her diminutive size, Eve Whitaker Slattery managed to fill the room. And she hadn't even stepped in yet. 'Sheriff, we demand to know what's going on. We understand our daughter's husband has been arrested.'

I didn't know if the 'we' meant she and her family or she was using the royal 'we'. I was betting on the latter.

Pavlik stood up. 'Mrs Slattery. Won't you come in?'

Eve Slattery stepped in and finally noticed me. 'Who's she?'

I was saved from answering by Stephen, who followed his mother in, and was trailed by a gray-haired man I assumed was his father.

'Mother,' Stephen said. 'I know you're upset, but don't be rude. This is Maggy Thorsen. I told you about her.'

'You're that man's first wife?' Mother Slattery advanced on me.

I stood up, more out of self-defense than politeness and stuck out my hand. 'I'm so sorry about Rachel.'

She slapped my hand away. 'You! If you had been half a woman, he wouldn't have gone after our Rachel.'

Wait a second here. 'I *am* half a . . . I mean, I know you're distraught, but—'

'Distraught? Distraught? Your husband kills my daughter and our only hope for a grandchild –' she threw a look at Stephen – 'and you wonder why I'm upset?'

'Now, Eve,' her husband said. The gentle-looking man apparently was used to being interrupted, because the preamble was all he had. He just left it at that and sat down in the chair next to me. His chair whistled, too.

'Excuse yourself, Andrew,' Mrs Slattery said.

'I didn't . . .' Again, he didn't finish the sentence.

I'd had about enough of these crazies. And I thought my family was dysfunctional. I'd pity Rachel if she wasn't already beyond that. As for Stephen, he had my sympathy.

'Why don't you take my chair,' I said to Mrs Slattery. 'I need to go.' Boy-oh-boy, did I need to go.

She didn't even acknowledge me as she hit back into Pavlik. I slipped past her to the doorway, where Stephen still stood.

I touched his shoulder. 'I'm so sorry about Rachel, Stephen.'

His eyes were already red and now they welled up. 'Thanks, Maggy, and please forgive my mo—'

'Stephen, would you please come over here. I need you.'

Stephen mouthed 'sorry' and stuck out his hand to shake. In it was his business card with his cellphone number scrawled on it.

'Call me if you need anything,' he said aloud. Then he reluctantly went to see what his mother wanted.

Me? I made a beeline for the door.

Eleven

Frank, faithful dog and companion, was waiting for me when I got home. We went through our usual routine before I stepped in. Me, unlocking the door, Frank crashing into the door. Same old, same old.

Once I wedged myself in, Frank did a little happy dance round and round as I attempted to scratch him behind the ear.

'That's a good boy, Frank. I'm glad to see you, too.'

Overwhelmed by love, the furry lug jumped up to put his paws on my shoulders. That placed him eye to eye with me.

His breath smelled of pigs' ears and he was drooling a bit, but all in all, he was the most appealing male I'd been with today, with the exception of Stephen.

'You're always glad to see me, aren't you, Frank?'

Frank gave a full-body wriggle and licked my nose. 'You love me no matter what. Don't you, boy?'

Another lick on the nose and another shimmy, this one strong enough to send a string of drool sailing.

Grateful as I was to inspire this kind of mindless adoration, I was a realist. I moved aside a hank of hair and looked him in the eye. 'You have to pee, don't you?'

Frank jumped down and ran for the door, woofing. So much for faithfulness and unconditional love, even from the canine set. All I was to him was the bathroom attendant.

By the time I got there, the dog stood squared up to the door, top of his head pressed against it, nose pointed down to the floor.

'You'll have to move back, if you want me to open it,' I told him.

He didn't move.

I turned the knob and managed to get it open a crack. Frank shuffled back an inch.

'More,' I said.

Another step. Or four, if you count all the feet.

At this rate, it was going to take an hour to get him out. 'You're an accident just waiting to happen,' I told him. 'Shove back.'

Another shuffle, but still no daylight between Frank's nose and the door.

Apparently Frank was frozen in the sheepdog equivalent of crossing your legs. I caught sight of his tennis ball behind the antique milk can I use as an umbrella stand.

I gave the ball a nudge with my toe and sent it rolling out from behind the milk can and away from us.

Frank instinctively started after the tennis ball, taking two steps before he realized he'd been tricked.

Before his bladder had a chance to figure it out, too, I yanked open the door. Frank threw me a grateful look and ran out.

'Whoa,' a voice outside said.

I stuck my head out and saw Stephen Slattery flattened up against the railing of the porch steps, looking after Frank.

'Sorry,' I said. 'Dog on a mission.'

'I can see that,' Stephen said, watching Frank water the red maple. 'Is he ever going to stop?'

'It's been a long day.' I stepped out on the porch. 'Longer for some than others. Want to come in?'

Stephen nodded and mounted the stairs, briefcase in hand.

'Wine?' I asked, and immediately flashed back to two days ago, when I'd asked his sister the same question. 'Or something else? Beer? Water? Coffee?'

'I had enough bad coffee at the sheriff's office.' He settled wearily on to the couch. Then, seeming to realize what he said, he added, 'Not that yours would be bad, of course. I'm sure being a . . . a . . . professional—'

'Believe me,' I interrupted, 'no offense taken.' I gestured toward the briefcase he was still holding. 'Do you want to put that down? Or do you want me to take it?'

Stephen looked at the case like he'd forgotten he still held it. Where his dark brown eyes had looked like glossy pools of chocolate when we'd met, now they looked dull.

'Sorry,' he said, handing the case to me. 'Your calendars are in here, the ones I didn't give to the sheriff.'

I opened the case. It looked like about three quarters of what I'd given him. Pretty much the first fifteen years of my marriage. 'Did they . . . I mean, did you . . .?' Now I was the one dithering.

Stephen leaned forward. 'After Rachel disappeared, I checked the last three years and found a couple discrepancies between the key cards and where your calendars said Ted was. I gave those to the sheriff.'

'And these?' I pulled out a handful of calendars.

'I didn't get a chance to check them, and I thought you would prefer they not have them.'

He was right about that. What was going on between Pavlik and me was bad enough without his having access to the mundane details of my life with Ted.

'Thanks,' I said, putting the calendars on the coffee table. 'I appreciate that. The sheriff—'

Stephen finished my thought. Or what he thought my thought was. 'I know. He already seems out to get Ted. No need to give him more fuel.'

I was startled. 'So you don't think Ted had anything to do with it?'

'Do you?'

I was still standing, empty briefcase in my hand. I handed it to him and collapsed in the chair opposite him.

'No,' I said, 'I honestly don't. It's just that . . .' I let it trail off.

'That he lied to you about Rachel and –' he waved at the calendars – 'and maybe other things.'

He saw my surprised look and smiled ruefully. 'Hey, think you're the only one? In poker terms, I see your cheating spouse and raise you a crazy mother.'

He reached across and touched my hand. 'I'm sorry she was so vile to you today. I'm so used to her that I don't notice until she launches into someone I like.'

He likes me, he really likes me, Sally Field screamed in my head. I ignored her. 'You were married?'

'For two years right out of college. My mother said Katrina was a tramp from the start.' He closed and unclosed the latch on his briefcase.

'And she was right?'

Stephen shrugged. 'Maybe. Or maybe being married to a Slattery made her want out in whatever way she could find.'

I didn't know what to say.

Stephen laughed. 'I know, I know. What a sad sack.'

Not a sad sack, so much as just plain sad. 'Sad sack?' I said, wanting to support his attempt to lighten the mood. 'I haven't heard that term for years.'

'I know, I'm a throwback. My dad had a collection of *Sad Sack* comic books I used to read.' He stood up. 'I'd better go.'

'So you and your father are close?' I asked, following him to the door.

'Sure. There's really nothing *not* to like about my dad,' Stephen said. 'My mother has worn him down for so many years, he's pretty much ceased to exist.'

'But you seem to have survived without losing yourself,' I said. 'And so did Rachel.'

'Rachel got away.' He was standing at the door.

'How? By marrying Ted?'

'Yes, and by choosing a career as far removed from the hotel business as she could manage. It worked for a while.'

'Just a while?'

'My mother said Rachel would be back and damned if she wasn't right.' Stephen gave me a rueful grin. 'Listen, I'm sorry to have unloaded like this on you. This was way more than you wanted to know about the Slattery clan.'

'The Family, with the capital "F"?' I asked, smiling. 'Don't worry. I've heard worse.'

'I find that hard to believe.'

He was looking at me, seeming more like he had before Rachel died. 'Would you have dinner with me tomorrow night?' he asked abruptly.

I must have looked surprised, because Stephen felt he had to explain. 'I know it might sound like terrible timing,' he said, 'but the next few days are bound to be pretty awful for everyone. It would be nice to get away for a few hours.'

'I—'

'It's just dinner,' he interrupted, and I realized that he was even more nervous than I was. 'And I swear –' he raised his hand appropriately – 'that I'll keep my crazy mother away.'

I waited two beats to make sure he was done. 'That it?'

'I think so. Unless you think a fiver would sweeten the deal.' He patted his wallet.

I grinned. 'I probably should wait to see if you up the ante, but the fact is I would love to have dinner.'

'You're a brave woman, Maggy,' Stephen said, a smile of relief spreading over his features. 'I'll call you tomorrow and we can work out the details.' With that, he pulled the door open.

Frank, his full bladder a distant memory, had been waiting impatiently on the porch. When the door finally opened, he was taking no chances. He threw himself in, sending Stephen, who still had hold of the door knob, hurtling backwards.

I was standing behind Stephen and a little to the side, so Frank didn't take me out. Heroically, though, I threw a body block to prevent Stephen from landing on the glass-topped coffee table. Instead, I sent him headlong over the arm of the couch, where he bounced and rolled to the floor between the sofa and the table.

Frank walked over him and settled next to the fireplace.

I looked down at Stephen apologetically. 'I guess we'll see who's brave.'

After I'd gotten Stephen up and brushed off, he still wanted to go to dinner. I thought this might be the man of my dreams.

Or at least my post-Pavlik dreams.

I worked with Amy the next day. This time, she had the 05:30 a.m. duties, so she was just finishing up the checklist when I got there at six thirty.

As Caron had done, I picked up the newspaper and tossed it on to the reading counter. When I did, I saw the headline: 'Body identified as Slattery heir.' The subhead read: 'Husband named person of interest.'

I scanned the story. Apparently dental records had confirmed that the body found in Lake Michigan was Rachel. The story didn't say what the cause of death was, only that the autopsy results were pending.

It went on to say that, according to sources close to the family, Rachel recently had announced her pregnancy. 'The sheriff's office would not say whether Slattery-Thorsen's husband, Brookhills' dentist Tor "Ted" Thorsen, was a suspect, but did say he was considered "a person of interest".'

Amy was peeking over my shoulder. 'Sounds like those other girls. The pregnant ones whose husbands killed them. It's an epidemic.'

I pointed at the paper. 'That's exactly the inference they want people to make. First the story says Rachel is dead, then that she's pregnant, and finally, that Ted is a suspect. What are people supposed to think?'

'It doesn't say he's a suspect,' Amy protested.

'I know. A person of interest.' I shook my head, turning to page six, where the article was continued. 'They might as well have said he was suspected. It's like when executives at the bank left to pursue other opportunities. We all knew damn well they'd been canned.'

'Isn't that you?' Amy pointed to a photo. It was shot through the glass of a car window and clearly showed me, in all my make-up-less glory. The caption under the picture read: 'Unidentified woman leaves house angrily Monday morning as questions are asked.'

'You do look angry,' Amy said. 'But at least they don't know who you are.'

'That will last as long as it takes someone from Brookhills to read the paper and pick up the telephone,' I said, tossing the paper in the trash basket. No use making it easier than it already was.

I took my handbag and coat back to the office and came

out with an Uncommon Grounds apron. '*Kat* McNamara is going to be all over this.'

Amy flipped around the open sign. 'Do you think it could have been suicide?'

I mulled over that possibility, which hadn't occurred to me until Eric asked me whether Rachel had jumped. 'I guess I assumed Pavlik has a reason to think it was murder, but I don't know whether that's true.'

'Caron said you saw Rachel the day she disappeared. Did she seem depressed to you?' Amy was sliding baskets full of pastry into the glass cabinet under the counter. 'Maybe she didn't want a baby.'

'Maybe.'

I hoped Caron wasn't repeating everything I'd told her. I didn't so much mind Amy knowing the particulars. Piercings and wind-chime earring aside, Amy had a good head on her shoulders. Even better, she had a good heart. There were some people in Brookhills, though, I couldn't say that about.

'I don't know whether Rachel wanted a baby,' I said, starting a latte, 'but she didn't seem suicidal to me. She was making plans.'

Most of those plans involved proving Ted was a cheater and kicking him out, not that I was going to tell Amy that.

'Plans for the baby?'

'There's construction work going on at the house and, according to Ted, it's for a nursery.'

I pushed the button to brew the espresso shot for my latte and turned back to Amy. 'Rachel didn't even tell me she was pregnant. I don't know if she was being considerate because she thought it would upset me or she figured it was none of my business.'

'Most likely the second, knowing Rachel.' Amy slid a latte cup over to me.

I was surprised. 'You've met Rachel?'

'We went to high school together. We weren't really friends. We ran in different circles.'

I was sure. Amy the tattooed, rainbow-haired, multiply-pierced environmentalist. Rachel, the well-coiffed blonde hotel heiress.

'Yeah, I was a cheerleader and ran track. Rachel was in the band and the chess club.'

I paused with the shot in my hand, about to pour it into the cup. 'You were a cheerleader and Rachel was the nerd?'

Amy took the shot from me and dumped it in the mug. 'We're human beings, Maggy. We evolve.'

She pointed at the big stainless frothing pitcher. 'You forgot to froth the milk. You're going to have to let it rest before you pour it.'

'You're right,' I said. 'On both counts.'

Properly chastised, I poured skim milk into the pitcher and positioned it under the steam wand. As the milk frothed, I tried to imagine Rachel throwing herself into the lake.

'I don't buy it,' I said, setting aside the milk to let it settle. As Amy had said, the milk has too much air in it right after frothing. If I used it in a drink, it would deflate, leaving me with a half-size latte. And a half-size latte wasn't enough.

'If Rachel wasn't thinking about the future,' I said to Amy, 'why would she have come to see me?'

'True.' Amy stirred a raw sugar into my latte mug. 'Caron told me about the key cards and all. Is that why you think Ted killed Rachel?'

No doubt about it, Caron had a big mouth. I hoped she'd only talked to Amy, but I'd think twice before I confided in her again. Sarah was the confessional by comparison.

'I don't think Ted killed anyone.' It wasn't the first time I'd said it, but this time I realized I meant it. I didn't think Ted had killed Rachel.

Why was that? Had something changed?

Not really. Except that since Rachel's body was found, I was no longer thinking in abstract terms.

Rachel was dead. Rachel. Not the 'Hotel Heiress' or even 'Ted's Tootsie'. Rachel. A person I knew.

And Ted was suspected of killing her. Ted. Not the 'Cheating Husband'. Ted. The man who had been the love of my life.

I might have to accept that he was a liar and a cheater. But I refused to believe he was a murderer.

Amy was pouring steamed milk into the espresso in my mug. She topped it with froth and handed it to me.

'So if you believe Ted is innocent,' she said matter-of-factly, 'aren't you going to help him prove it?'

Twelve

Yet another good question. One that I thought about as I dodged reporters with questions about why I'd been at Ted's house. The *CitySentinel* must be very happy with its circulation numbers in Brookhills.

'I'd kill to find out who called the paper,' I said to Amy mid-morning.

'It was that frickin' Roger Karsten,' Sophie called over from the table in the corner.

I pulled a fresh pot of coffee off the heating element and went over to Sophie's table. 'Refill?' I asked, and then realized she didn't have a cup.

'I'm just visiting,' she said.

It must be hell getting old and having your trip to the coffee shop be the high point of your day. Then again, it was often the high point of *my* day. Frank was cute, but he sure wasn't much of a conversationalist.

I got a cup and poured some coffee in it, sliding it in front of Sophie. 'On the house,' I said. 'Now, how do you know it was Roger?'

'I heard him tell that Kat woman.'

Great.

'Speak of the devil,' Amy said from behind the counter. 'Kate is crossing the parking lot and it looks like she's coming our way.'

'Dang, Maggy,' Sophie exclaimed, 'hide!'

It seemed like good advice. Being careful to stay away from the window, I slid around the corner and into the office.

'That's the first place she'll look,' Sophie called.

She was right, but the only other place to go was the refrigerator.

Or outside. I let myself out the back door and into the service corridor. I could stay there but if Kate checked the office, she certainly would check the hall. Better to slip out when she's still looking for me inside. I could go to Sarah's office.

I opened the door that led into the back parking lot.

'Slick,' Kate's voice said. 'You might have fooled a lesser woman.' Kate was leaning casually against the building wall.

'How in the world did you get back here so fast?' I asked disgustedly. 'You couldn't have seen me.'

'You have one full wall of mirrors,' Kate said. 'I saw your reflection as you slunk into the back.'

Defeated by my own need to make Uncommon Grounds look spacious.

'Those mirrors were a crappy idea in the first place,' I muttered. 'Fingerprints.'

Kate whipped out her 'Ace Reporter' notebook. The decoder ring was probably back at the office. 'What were you doing at your ex-husband's house the night his wife disappeared?'

I bit back the smart-aleck remark that would have been fun, but probably unwise.

'Take a hike, Kate,' I said, walking away from her. Today was another mild day, so I wasn't suffering from the cold in my jeans and Uncommon Grounds T-shirt.

'C'mon, Maggy,' Kate said, trailing me, 'give me something, will you? Please?'

I stopped and turned. 'Please? You said please?' It was nearly as unusual as seeing Sarah's legs.

Kate gestured with her notebook. 'I would kill to write for the *CitySentinel*. If I could get something, *any*thing from you, it would be a real coup for me.'

I still hesitated, so she pulled out her ace in the hole. 'C'mon, Maggy. Do you *truly* want me to stay in Brookhills the rest of my career?'

That did it. I waved her over. 'Thing is, Kate. There's really nothing to tell.'

'That's what they all say.' She flipped open her notebook. 'So are you and your ex back together? Is that why he killed his new wife?'

I stepped back. Years of doing public relations taught me many lessons. One of them was controlling the interview. 'I'll give you a statement, but I'm not going to answer any questions.'

Kate opened her mouth to protest, but I was insistent. 'This isn't negotiable.' I nodded at her notebook. 'Are you ready?'

She raised the notebook and had the pen poised.

'Ted Thorsen and I have an amicable divorce, but we have absolutely no intention of reuniting. From everything I've seen, he loved Rachel and is shocked and heartbroken over her death. He called me the morning after she disappeared, because he was upset and had no other family to call. I went to try to help. End of statement.'

I turned on my heel. Kate was still scribbling as the service door closed behind me.

'Did you get rid of her?' Amy asked as I entered the store.

'I did.' I looked around. 'Where did Sophie go?'

'When she saw Kate circle the building she said she was going to go out and "tail" her.'

'That's good.' I picked up the tray of dirty cups and plates to load them in the dishwasher. 'I think Sophie could use a little excitement in her life.'

Amy leaned over to help me. 'I don't think that's all Sophie needs.'

I pulled back and looked at Amy. 'Are you talking about her and Henry?'

Amy laughed and flipped up the door of the dishwasher. 'No, I'm talking about money. Most seniors are living on a fixed income. Haven't you noticed how she comes around for the leftover bakery at night?'

'I hadn't, but Caron mentioned it to me.' I surveyed our assortment of delicious, yet not nutritious pastry. 'I hope she's not living on this stuff. Maybe we should get some wholegrains in here.'

Amy grinned. '*Now* you're talking.' Amy was a natural and organic foods devotee.

I put my hand on her arm. 'You truly don't think Sophie's in serious financial trouble, do you?'

'Not serious, but I think she has to watch her pennies. It can't be easy living in Brookhills, surrounded by people who buy whatever they want without a second thought.'

I got that. Business-owner or not, I made well below the average income in Brookhills. Heck, it was *because* I was a business owner. When I was working for somebody else, I did just fine.

It was the price you pay for following your own drummer. Right into the poorhouse.

Amy left before I did, but as I hung up my apron at six, I was still thinking about the question she had asked me about Ted.

If I believed he was innocent, shouldn't I do what I could to help him prove that?

Yes, I knew that Ted wasn't my problem anymore. But I couldn't get over the look on his face as Pavlik had led him away. Ted was alone.

What about Emma Byrne? the voice in my head asked. Let *her* help him.

A fair question, Voice in Head. But if Rachel had been right about the affair, then Emma's help was the last thing Ted needed. Much like me being photographed at his house and plastered all over the newspaper.

But at least no one could prove that Ted and I were together because we simply *weren't*. Emma, on the other hand . . .

If they were having an affair, Emma's riding to his rescue would only prove Ted had a motive for getting rid of Rachel. But why would he choose to do it now, if he and Emma had been . . . affairing for years?

I grabbed my purse in one hand and a bag of trash in the other and headed out the back door, still noodling it.

Money was the logical motive. Presumably Ted would inherit everything Rachel had. But how much was there? And what about the prenup Rachel had mentioned? Did that enter in? I didn't know.

I was saved the trouble of digging out my key to the dumpster corral because the lock hadn't been fixed and the gate was hanging open. Trash pickup wasn't until Friday, so the computer monitors, box spring and paint cans were still there, too. Happily, the scary man didn't appear to be.

Even so, I was cautious as I stepped in. Setting down my purse, I climbed up on a slat of the box spring and swung the heavy garbage bag into our dumpster. The truck-size trash bin was stenciled 'UG' for Uncommon Grounds, not that the identification was necessary. I would have been able to identify it blindfolded, because of the stench. I love the smell of fresh-brewed coffee. Moldy grounds are a different story.

Retrieving my purse, I swung the dumpster gate closed behind me. It creaked back open. I shrugged. At least I'd tried to be a good dumpster doobie. Caron would be proud.

When I rounded the corner to the front parking lot, I checked my watch. Six fifteen. I was meeting Stephen at the hotel restaurant at eight. That gave me just enough time to get home, shower, dress and drive downtown.

I was looking forward to dinner. Not only would I be eating at what was reputed to be a wonderful restaurant, but I would be doing it – *eating*, that is – with a handsome man who was both interesting and, seemingly, interested.

And if that weren't enough, Stephen probably also had the answers to a whole lot of my questions.

Chez Slattery (geez, did these people love the sound of their own name or what?) was on the top floor of the Slattery Arms.

Stephen met me at the door. He was wearing a dark suit and though he looked tired, his eyes sparkled when he saw me. Given the circumstances, it had been tough to know how to dress. I'd chosen an LBD – Little Black Dress. Good for any occasion. Wedding, funeral, dinner, interrogation.

'You look wonderful,' he said, leaning down to give me a peck on the cheek.

'Thank you.' I gestured at the floor to ceiling windows. 'The view is fabulous.'

'You've never been here before?' He signaled the hostess we were ready to be seated.

'Not for years and years,' I admitted.

The hostess led us past the bar to a separate section, apparently for VIPs of some sort. There were only four tables in an area that would have held twice that number in the main area of Chez Slattery. Two of the tables were unoccupied. At the third, a well-preserved older blonde chatted with a man who looked about fifteen years her junior. I almost applauded when I walked past.

I sat down in the chair the hostess was holding and she placed my napkin on my lap. 'The last time I was here, the restaurant still . . .' I made a circling motion with my finger.

'Ahh, revolved. It was all the rage for a while. Now people seem to prefer not to rotate while they digest.'

'You're telling me. I was very young and not much of a drinker. Between the martinis my date was ordering for me and the motion, I don't remember much.'

'And what you do remember, you'd rather not.' Stephen smiled from across the table.

'True.' Especially the last couple of years. My 'date' that night had been Ted. It was the first time we went out and he was trying to impress me.

I looked out the window. 'This is absolutely lovely.'

It was. We were looking east. At our feet, the Milwaukee River sliced through the lights of the city, delineated by the harp lights of the Riverwalk.

East Town lay on the other side of the river, its restaurants and clubs hopping, car lights zipping in and out as valets maneuvered patrons' cars into parking spots. Beyond that, I could see the illuminated Brise Soleil, the moving sunscreen that architect Santiago Calatrava had designed to top his first building in the United States, the Quadracci Pavilion of the Milwaukee Art Museum.

'Oh, look,' I said pointing at the Brise. 'It's opening. I thought they closed it at night.'

'I think the Art Museum has a fundraiser tonight,' Stephen said, as we watched the wings unfurl dramatically like a huge bird – a bird with a two-hundred-foot wingspan – against the blackness that was Lake Michigan.

The lake sparkled with sunlight on nice days and seemed as unforgiving as the ocean on stormy ones. At night, though, it was simply emptiness. The cliff, where the city lights fell away. Dark. Cold. Empty.

The place where Rachel had died.

I craned my head to look north.

'What are you looking for?' Stephen asked as he took the wine list from the sommelier.

'The Hamilton,' I said, without thinking.

'There,' he pointed. 'The big cream-colored one. Why?'

The Hamilton was about six blocks west of the lake, and that didn't take into account the parkland, which created another buffer of two or three blocks, depending where you were on the lakefront.

I turned to Stephen. 'Rachel was going to the Hamilton. However did she end up in the lake?'

Stephen's eyes were as bleak as the lake now. I was sorry to be the cause of it, but there was no way we could dance around his sister's death.

'I've been trying to figure that out myself,' he said. 'Apparently she had on the same clothes she was wearing on Saturday when they found . . .' He swallowed hard. 'Her body.'

I put my hand out to cover his. 'I'm so sorry, Stephen. I wish I could help.'

He squeezed my hand. 'You are, believe me. Just being here and talking through all this is a tremendous help. My mother doesn't want to try to make sense of this. She just wants someone punished.'

Like Ted, for example. If this was helping Stephen, I was glad. It was helping me, too, besides being awfully pleasant. 'I understand Rachel never showed up to meet the inspector.'

Stephen leaned forward. 'Really? Who told you that?'

'The inspector himself. Roger Karsten used to be the Brookhills' building inspector and now has his own inspection firm,' I said. 'He said he'd had an appointment to meet Rachel at the Hamilton.'

We were interrupted by the sommelier. 'Sorry.' Stephen picked up the wine list. 'Do you prefer red or white?'

'Red, please. I know I should decide based on what I order, but I like red with just about anything.'

'Me, too.' He scanned the wine list. 'I think we'll have a French Bordeaux.'

He pointed at one. The sommelier nodded his approval and then took the list and himself back to . . . wherever sommeliers come from.

'When did you see this inspector?' Stephen asked.

'He came into Uncommon Grounds yesterday. He hasn't been around for months, so this was the first time I've heard from him.'

'And he just stopped by the coffeehouse out of the blue?' Stephen sounded doubtful.

It did seem odd when you put it like that. On the other hand . . . 'Roger is pretty full of himself. I wouldn't put it past him to make a special trip just to let people know he'd been interviewed by the police.'

Stephen rubbed his chin. 'I assume he'd know that you're Ted's ex-wife.'

I snorted and the couple at the next table turned. Apparently people didn't snort in Chez Slattery.

'Sorry,' I said, putting my hand over my mouth. 'It's just that everyone knows what and who everybody is doing in Brookhills.'

Stephen smiled at that. 'Do you think he might have been looking for information, rather than giving it? Maybe he was curious.'

There was that. 'He didn't ask me anything, though he did get sidetracked.' By Laurel's boobs, if I recalled.

'Did he say how long he waited for her?'

'Fifteen minutes, which is quintessential Roger. He waits for no man. Or woman.'

'Municipal inspectors can get away with that and, to be fair, they're often on a tight schedule. But a private inspector usually will wait if a client – especially one as big as Slattery Hotels – gets hung up.'

'I can see that. That would be the only way he'd get paid, after all. Though by Roger's standards, fifteen minutes *is* waiting. I wonder if he tried to call her.'

'Maybe. But if he called Rachel's cellphone, we'll never know. It was lost.'

Like Rachel and the baby were 'lost'.

'The sheriff probably has already checked the records,' I said.

'I wish we knew where she was going after her meeting at the Hamilton,' Stephen said.

'Did she keep a calendar or a datebook?'

'On the phone, probably. It was new, and she was pretty addicted to it.' He mustered up a smile.

The blessing of all-in-one handheld technology is also its curse. Everything could be wiped out all at once. Phone, address book, calendar, the whole shebang. And we are as dependent on that information as we are our cars.

Which reminded me. 'Where is Rachel's SUV?' The Escalade shouldn't be hard to spot. It was the size of a bus.

'Nobody has seen it yet. The sheriff says that if the killer left it unlocked in the right part of town, it wouldn't last twenty minutes before it ended up in the chop shop. I wonder if anyone saw her when she stopped back here.'

'Here?'

'Not here at the restaurant, but the office.'

'How do you know that? Did someone see her?'

He shook his head. 'No, I'm only assuming she came back, because of the key cards they found in her purse. She must have taken them from the office.'

That explained why Rachel had 'more' key cards. They weren't *more*. They were the same ones.

'Does Pavlik have any other suspects except Ted?' I asked.

Stephen shifted uncomfortably in his chair.

I held up my hand. 'That's OK, you don't have to say anything. It's just . . .' My fingers were drumming nervously on the table.

'I'm sorry,' Stephen said, covering my hand this time. 'I know this is hard on you, too. "It's just" what?'

'Just . . . I don't know what evidence they have. In fact, I don't know if they're absolutely certain Rachel was murdered.' I looked into his dark eyes. 'Is there any chance it was suicide?'

Stephen's face crumpled. 'I thought of that. I don't believe Rachel would kill herself. But with the pregnancy and the situation with Ted and all . . . who knows?'

'If she decided she didn't want the baby, might she have considered an abortion?' I asked.

'Never,' Stephen said. 'My mother would have killed her.'

He realized what he'd said and held up his hand. 'Figure of speech.'

'I know,' I assured him. 'But I assume your mother wants grandchildren.'

'More heirs, than grandchildren. But, yes. And she knows she's not going to get them from me.'

'No?'

'Nope. Vasectomy when I was twenty-one.' Stephen turned a little red in the face, but he plunged on, looking down at the table. 'Rachel and I used to call ourselves hostages to the Slattery fortune. Who would wish that on our kids?'

'Whatever are you talking about, Stephen?'

Eve Whitaker Slattery was at my elbow. I pulled it off the table.

'Why is she here?' she demanded, apparently meaning me.

Now, I'll be honest. Mother Slattery scared the snot out of me. Any minute I expected a second set of incisors to telescope out of her Botoxed lips and devour me, à la *Alien*.

Still, no one calls me 'she'. Not when I'm sitting right there.

'*She*,' I said, 'is having dinner with *he*.' I pointed at Stephen.

'She is,' Stephen agreed solemnly.

'While your sister lies dead at the hands of her husband?' The fact that she was pointing a well-manicured finger at me indicated that the 'her' was me.

'Mother, I told you—'

'First of all,' I said standing to take advantage of the three or so inches I had on her, 'he is not my husband, he is . . . was Rachel's husband. Secondly,' I continued, before she could interrupt, 'I don't believe Ted had anything to do with Rachel's death.'

I was at a loss for the slam-dunk third point, so I sat back down, picked up the napkin that had fallen when I stood up and smoothed it across my lap.

Stephen cleared his throat. 'Actually, Mother, we were just talking about Rachel. Since Maggy and I were the last ones to see her alive, we were trying to piece together what we know.'

We were? I was sort of hoping this was a date – an insensitively timed one, perhaps, but a date nonetheless. Even if I had planned to pump Stephen for information, myself.

'In fact,' Stephen continued pointedly, 'Maggy was just asking me if I thought that Rachel could have killed herself.'

Mrs Slattery held up her hands to quiet Stephen, looking around to make sure no one had heard. 'That is . . . is . . .' For the first time, a crack appeared in the classy facade.

Eve abruptly stepped over and jerked a chair away from the other occupied table. Placing it at ours, she sat down. The blonde at the table tore herself away from playing footsie with her companion long enough to look up, annoyed. Seeing who the chair-stealer was, though, she shut her mouth and went back to Junior.

'Rachel would never kill herself,' Eve hissed. 'Not over that husband of hers. She was a stronger woman than that. Besides, she had the baby to think about. That child was our only chance to pass on the family name, God knows.'

I met Stephen's eyes, but he seemed unaffected. Apparently he was accustomed to his mother's jibes.

'When was Rachel due?' I asked.

'October,' Mrs Slattery said. 'The baby would have been born in late October.'

I did a little mental arithmetic. It had been a while since I'd figured out due dates and such. 'So she was less than three months along,' I said. 'Maybe more like two and a half.'

'Excuse me.'

Yet another unwanted visitor at my elbow. This one was Pavlik. 'I don't mean to interrupt, but Mr Slattery said I could find you here.' He was speaking to Eve Slattery.

'I hope you've come to tell me you've charged that man with murder.' She threw me a look.

'I'm afraid just the opposite,' Pavlik said. 'The Milwaukee district attorney didn't have enough to hold Mr Thorsen. We had to let him go. I wanted to tell you in person.'

I knew Pavlik well enough to know that telling her in person, especially in a public place, hadn't been his idea. Maybe the county executive or some bigwig in the DA's office, but not Pavlik.

'You *what*? You let the man who murdered my daughter go free?' She wasn't actually yelling, but she still had the attention of the couple next door. I also caught sight of a head peeking over the foliage that separated us from the common folk.

Pavlik tried to calm her down. 'Since the crime must have occurred in Milwaukee, it wasn't up to me or to anyone else in Brookhills County. But even if it had been, I don't think there's currently enough evidence—'

Eve Whitaker Slattery rose to her full five foot two. 'Don't *you* think for a moment, young man, that your district attorney and county executive won't be hearing about this. Stephen – come with me,' she said imperiously, and swept off.

Stephen stood up. 'I appreciate your coming by and letting us know personally,' he said to Pavlik. Then he turned to me. 'I should probably go and do damage control. For everyone's sake.'

'Of course,' I said. 'Go.'

Pavlik and I watched Stephen hurry out, stopping only at the hostess stand for a hurried conversation. Presumably he was making sure I wouldn't be left with the bill. Not that it hadn't been worth the price of admission.

Show over, the blonde and Junior headed for the bar.

Pavlik sank into the chair Mrs Slattery had vacated.

'Never give women bad news in public places,' I said, pouring wine into an empty water glass for him.

'I thought it was supposed to keep them quiet,' he muttered, picking up his wine and setting it back down again without drinking.

Sandra Balzo

'It doesn't work.' I took a sip of my wine.

'No shit.' Pavlik eyed me. 'You are just all over this case. You want to tell me why you're here?'

'I'm a friend of Stephen's and we were having dinner.'

'You just met Stephen three days ago and you were pumping him for information.'

That, too. 'Only because I didn't have you to pump.'

Pavlik didn't rise to the bait. In fact, I didn't think Pavlik would be rising in my vicinity anytime soon. He pushed back from the table and spread his hands. 'You have questions? Ask me.'

His eyes weren't blue, but they weren't nearly as black as the lake beyond the lights of the city, either. They were official gray – dirty Chevy gray, I had called them when we first met. Not to his face, of course.

'OK,' I said, pushing back my chair to try to match his level of detachment. 'Isn't it possible that Rachel committed suicide?'

'No.'

'You know that for a fact?'

'I know that for a fact.'

For someone who offered to answer questions, he wasn't being very forthcoming. 'How?'

He pushed the chair back even farther. 'Because suicides don't beat themselves in the face, kick themselves in the stomach, die, and then jump in the water.' He stood up. 'Any other questions?'

Nope. That should about do it.

Thirteen

Rachel, pregnant, had been beaten in the face and kicked in the stomach. On television they would say that indicated a crime of passion. That the killer was someone who knew her well.

It was an absolutely hideous crime and I could understand Mrs Slattery's anger at Ted's release. No one else had been implicated. If Ted hadn't killed Rachel, who had?

I let Frank out when I got home and went to the computer. Returning and sensing my mood, he lay down quietly next to my chair as I logged into e-mail.

I'd tried not to involve Eric in too much of this, but I really wanted to 'talk' to him now. E-mail or instant message would be perfect, since it would give me time to consider my answers before I pressed 'send'.

But my 'E-Buddy' icon indicated Eric wasn't online, which meant he was out. That was OK. We always had texting.

I punched in: 'How's everything?' Eric had explained to me that I didn't have to use a salutation, like 'Hi Eric' or a signature like 'Love you, Mom', because the phone only belonged to one person and the message indicated who it was from. Even so, I added the 'Love you' part every time. I'm still a mom.

I'd barely had time to set down the cellphone before it beeped. 'New text' showed in the window. I pressed 'View'.

'Anything new on rachel'

I sat there for a second looking at the screen. The only thing new was that I knew how she died. I didn't want to tell him that. Not now.

I pressed in: 'Not that I know.'

'Ok ill check with dad'

At least Ted had been released, so he could text back. 'Need anything?' I asked.

'Im broke can you transfer money'

I turned back to the computer and brought up the screen with our accounts on them. Sure enough, his checking account was down to $4.03. His available balance was '$.03.' Good cash flow management.

I transferred fifty dollars from my not-so-flush-itself checking account into his. Then I punched in: 'Just transferred fifty. Make it last. Love you.'

I hit 'send'.

A minute later: 'Thanks i get said Friday'

As I said, texting isn't perfect. The word was supposed to be 'paid' not 'said'.

The 'love you' that followed, though, came through just fine.

I surfed and did e-mail for a couple more hours. As I started to shut down the computer, I noticed that my e-mail box for 'MTEThorsen', my pre-divorce screen name (Maggy, Ted, Eric – MTE – get it? Clever, no?), had 893 e-mails in it. When I'd created my new account 'NoTed', I hadn't closed out the old one, figuring the forwarded jokes and Viagra ads needed a place to call their own. I tried to clean it out regularly, but it had been a while.

I double-clicked the icon and the list loaded, newest e-mails at the top.

The most recent subject line was 'Buy OEM Software'.

What in the world was OEM software and why did everyone on the Internet want to sell it to me? I pushed delete.

Next down, I was invited to 'Make all your wishes come true' and, below that, 'Stop smoking today!'. Sandwiched between 'Check out the e-card a friend sent you!' and 'Ashamed of your size? Megadik can help!' was an e-mail address I recognized.

Ted's.

I double-clicked it open. The header contained the e-mail address of pretty much anyone Ted had ever met. It was the list he used to forward jokes. But this was no joke.

'I'm sorry,' the message read, 'but I can't go to jail. I love you all. Goodbye.' It was signed simply 'Ted'.

The time stamp said it had been sent at four forty-five this afternoon. I'd barely finished reading it when my cell-phone rang.

'Mom?'

'Eric?' I checked the clock. Midnight. And he was calling, not texting.

'Mom, I texted Dad and didn't hear back. I checked e-mail when I got home and I have this hinky one from him.'

'I know,' I said, 'I just opened it, too. I don't want you to worry. I'll call and make sure everything's OK.'

'I tried, both the cell and the house. And I texted. He's not answering.' I could hear the panic brimming in my son's voice, ready to spill over. 'What is Dad sorry about? Why would he be going to jail?'

I didn't know what to say. I hadn't told Eric that Rachel's death had been a murder and that Ted was a suspect. I guess I'd hoped I wouldn't have to.

'What aren't you telling me?' he demanded.

'I'm sorry, Eric, but I guess I was trying to protect you. Rachel was . . . killed.' Was that weenie enough for you?

My kid's no weenie, though. 'Killed? You mean Rachel was murdered? Is that why Dad says he can't go to jail? Do the cops think Dad killed her?'

'I . . . I think they do.'

'What a load of crap.'

Suddenly Eric sounded like a man, instead of the scared child I'd heard in his voice. Who was I kidding? The scared child I heard in my own voice.

'I know, but—' I started.

'Does he have a good lawyer?' Eric interrupted. 'Did you get him a good lawyer?'

Ted was no longer my responsibility. I knew that and Eric knew that. But if I abandoned Ted now, it was like abandoning Eric. And even if I was afraid that part of my married life was a lie, it sure didn't include Eric.

'I'm going over there right now,' I said. 'I will find him. If he doesn't have a lawyer, I will make sure he gets one.'

But that wasn't my biggest worry now. My biggest worry was that Ted's note was a true goodbye. As in, forever. I was afraid that I was going to find Ted dead in the beautiful home on Wildwood Drive.

'Mom?' The little boy was back in his voice.

'Yes, sweetie?' I was digging through my purse for my car keys, the cellphone stuck between my ear and my shoulder.

'You think he's OK, right?' He cleared his throat. 'I mean, Dad wouldn't . . .?'

'No, he wouldn't,' I said firmly. 'Not your father. Not ever.'

I guess you never stop trying to protect your kids.

The first thing I noticed as I pulled around a parked car and turned into the driveway of the house was that the Miata was gone.

The second was that there were no lights. It wouldn't necessarily have concerned me, but not even the front porch light was on.

Since there are no streetlights on any of the residential streets in Brookhills, most people leave their front lights on all night to provide some illumination. A totally dark house is an invitation to burglars, even in the quietest neighborhoods. Actually, especially in the quietest neighborhoods.

As I pulled up the driveway, my Escape didn't trigger the motion-sensitive floodlights on each side of the garage door either. Despite the fact the neighbors were exactly four-tenths of an acre away on each side (Brookhills building regs), I was spooked as I got out of the car.

Closing the car door as quietly as I could, I felt like I was the trespasser. And I was. While my son would have a right to be here, I had zero standing now – zip.

Weird how two people who swore to 'forsake all others' could simply walk away, but their kids were stuck with their parents and *their* respective families forever. Stephen Slattery could worry about his kids becoming hostages to the Slattery fortune, but that sure beat being hostage to Ted's mom's lutefisk every Christmas.

It was silent as I approached the house. The classic night sounds of southeastern Wisconsin suburbia – the wind in the trees, the hoot-hoot of the Great Horned Owls, the swish-swish of the in-ground sprinkling systems – all were eerily absent.

Not even a yapping chihuahua to be found. I was still hoping, though, that Ted would open the door as I stepped up on to the porch.

He didn't. Not even leaning on the doorbell for the count of twenty got any reaction from either Ted or ChiChi. I stepped around a cedar planter to reach the window. The smell of peat moss and soil wafted up from the container as I peered in. Rachel must have been getting ready to plant.

I could only make out shapes in the living room. Most of them looked benign enough. Couches, chairs, tables, lamps. No huddled bodies on the floor. No silhouetted chandeliers swinging under the weigh—

A hand dropped on my shoulder. I whirled, letting my training take over. 'Fire!' I screamed.

Pavlik looked at me. 'Fire?'

'Geez,' I said, putting my hand to my chest. 'You scared the hell out of me.'

'But "fire"?' Pavlik repeated.

'That's what you're supposed to yell when you're attacked,' I explained. 'People pay more attention to that than "help".'

'True,' Pavlik said. 'Especially sheriff's deputies with guns.'

Pavlik signaled and a floodlight illuminated the front of the house. The light came from the car I'd seen parked when I turned into the driveway. There were ten or twelve deputies surrounding the house with their hands on their gun holsters.

Lucky I hadn't yelled 'ready, aim' before I screamed 'fire'. 'You had the house staked out?'

Pavlik shrugged. 'Homicide suspect. We like to keep track of them.'

I gestured at the men watching us. 'You need a dozen deputies and the sheriff for that?'

'No, we had two deputies in the car. The rest came with me.'

I was trying to see his eyes, but since his back was to the light, they looked like black pits. Gave me the creeps.

'You heard about the e-mail?' I hazarded.

'Stephen Slattery is on your husband's joke list. As, apparently, are you.' His tone made it clear that he didn't consider this a joke either.

'*Ex*-husband,' I corrected automatically, even though I knew from experience that Pavlik was just working me. 'I picked up the message about a half hour ago.'

'You should have called it in.'

'I know,' I admitted, and I did know. I just didn't *do*. 'But Eric called me in a panic.'

'Your son was on the list, too?' I heard concern in his voice. Pavlik had met Eric only once, but the two had hit it off. Even if they hadn't, Pavlik wouldn't like the idea of a kid getting news like that.

'I had to tell him the whole story. Then I came over here to look for Ted. I . . . Eric was afraid that—'

'That his father had killed himself,' Pavlik finished.

'Yes.' I was uncomfortably aware of all the time we were wasting. 'Now can't you break the door down or something?'

'We could,' Pavlik said as a deputy strode up the driveway toward us, 'but it would be easier to use a key. I had someone stop by Stephen Slattery's place and pick up a spare his sister left with him.'

'Good. Then use it.' I nodded toward the door.

Pavlik took the key from the deputy. I couldn't see the eye-roll exchange, so much as feel it.

'Now, please?' I followed Pavlik over to the door and watched as he unlocked it. When he pushed it open, I went to follow him in. The deputy blocked me.

'Pavlik?' I called after the sheriff. 'He's not letting me in.'

'I know,' Pavlik's voice, moving away, said.

'I have a right to go in.' I was trying to sound 'assertive', but getting 'tearful'. I cleared my throat. 'I was married to Ted for twenty years.'

'I'm well aware of that.' Pavlik stuck his head back out

and his voice softened. 'That's exactly why you can't come in.'

'Did you find him?' I asked fearfully.

'No, but I've only gotten into the foyer, so far.'

He signaled and four deputies, three men and a woman, came forward. I stepped back to let them through.

'You don't want me to see . . .' I hesitated. 'Him.'

'Were you going to say "his body"?' Pavlik stepped out and drew me aside, leaving his deputies to search. 'That e-mail could just as likely be a goodbye to his friends, as a suicide note.'

'A goodbye?'

'As in, "I have to leave for now. See you later." You know, a goodbye.'

I peered up at him. 'That's what goodbye means to you?'

'Sure. What else?'

I didn't answer that. 'So why would he run?'

Pavlik looked me in the eye. 'Because he's guilty.'

'Or afraid.' I stared right back at him.

The stare-down was interrupted by the female deputy. 'There's nobody here, sheriff. It looks like he took off.'

This time I trailed Pavlik in, noting that all the lights had been flipped on. I was glad to see that Brookhills' investigators didn't walk around in the dark with flashlights like TV cops did.

'Looks like he took the computer,' the deputy was saying. 'The docking station for the laptop is empty.'

Pavlik shook his head. 'How the hell did he get out of here without the guys out front seeing?'

'The back?' I suggested under my breath.

Pavlik threw me a dirty look.

'An officer noted a Miata parked illegally earlier,' the deputy said sheepishly. 'It was one street over.'

'Let me guess: it's gone now?' Pavlik asked, disgusted. The deputy just nodded.

'All the lights were out when I arrived,' I said. 'If he stayed in the shadows along the house—'

Pavlik interrupted, 'What else is missing?' he asked the deputy.

'Probably some clothes. Things are thrown all over the bedroom upstairs like he was packing.'

'Or maybe someone was searching for something?' I was looking into the kitchen. 'The pantry door is open and cereal is all over the floor.'

Pavlik threw me an annoyed look, but stepped into the kitchen. Bending down, he examined the spill.

'Krispees?' I asked.

'More like Friskies.' Pavlik straightened up with a piece in his hand. 'This is dog food.'

I squinted at it. 'It's too small.'

Pavlik snorted. 'You're feeding a small horse. They were feeding a big rat.'

I looked around. 'So where *is* the rat?'

'Must be with Thorsen,' the deputy said, coming into the room.

'Homicidal maniacs usually take their chihuahuas when they skip town?' I asked.

Pavlik and the deputy looked at each other.

'Lonely homicidal maniacs, maybe,' Pavlik tried.

Yeah. And they pack them doggy bags, too.

Pavlik was already on his cellphone, probably putting an APB out.

'Tell them to follow the trail of Kibbles and Bits,' I suggested.

The deputy stifled a laugh and headed back to the bedroom, taking the stairs two at a time.

'Sorry,' I said, when Pavlik flipped the phone closed.

'Sorry for what?'

'Undermining your authority.'

This time, it was Pavlik who laughed and he didn't bother to stifle it. 'It's going to take more than a dog food joke to undermine my authority, Maggy. These people are glad to have me. They worked for a sheriff who ate himself to death, remember?'

I did. Sadly, the doughnut-loving cop stereotype was all too true in Sheriff Niebuhr's case. 'Jelly doughnuts don't kill people,' I intoned solemnly. 'People kill people.'

Another grin from Pavlik. I was making progress here.

And I was so relieved that Ted had not committed suicide by doughnut or anything else, that I hadn't really thought about the obvious question.

Pavlik did though. 'So where would he go, Maggy?' He was standing close to me.

'I honestly don't know.'

Pavlik took me by the shoulders. 'Think about it. Did Ted say anything? Did he give you any indication why he did this?'

Did this? 'You mean run away?'

Pavlik kept his gaze steady. 'I mean, kill his wife.'

I tried to move back, but he kept the light insistent pressure on my shoulders.

Pavlik is half a foot taller than I am, lean and muscular. At this moment he could choose to pull me to him and kiss me thoroughly, or he could slide his hands together and crush my larynx.

It was one of the things that fascinated me most about him.

And frightened me.

I put my hands on his chest and pushed back hard. 'Ted did not kill Rachel.'

I didn't so much as budge him, but he dropped his hands. 'I know you want to believe that.'

'I *do* believe that.'

'And you don't know where he would run.'

I shook my head. 'No.'

'Would you tell me if you knew?'

'Of course, it would be a crime not to. Withholding information, right?'

'Right. Spousal privilege does not attach to ex-wives.'

Pavlik meant that I could be forced to testify against Ted now, though that wasn't true when we were married.

'You've never hesitated to withhold information before, spousal or otherwise,' Pavlik pointed out.

Low blow. And they say women are always bringing up the past.

I opened my mouth, but Pavlik's cellphone rang.

As he listened to the person on the other end, I was busy framing my reply.

Unfortunately, I never got a chance.

'I'm sorry, Maggy.' Pavlik slid the phone back in the pocket of his jacket.

'Sorry? What happened? Is Ted OK?'

My God, I'd divorced the man for cheating on me and here I was blithering for fear something had happened to him. Did this make any sense at all?

But Pavlik shook his head. 'That was our numbers guy. Apparently, Ted went online just before five yesterday afternoon and transferred all the money from his and his wife's joint accounts.'

'Five o'clock? But that was just after . . .'

'He wrote the e-mail.' Pavlik stepped closer, so close I had to tilt my head to look up at him. 'He sent the e-mail, emptied all the accounts, including—'

I started to interrupt and Pavlik held up a finger. 'Including one with four hundred thousand dollars in it from the sale of some of Rachel's Slattery stock. It was money she'd planned to spend on an addition to the house, according to her brother.'

'The nursery,' I said, not daring to breathe. Or maybe the nursery *wing*, at that price. None of this made any sense.

'Yes.' He put his hands on my shoulders again. 'He killed his pregnant wife by battering her face and tossing her into Lake Michigan. Then he stole the money she'd put aside for the baby's nursery, plus everything else they had that was liquid – a total of about half a million – and ran.'

He put his index finger under my chin and forced me to look up at him. 'I know it's hard to believe that the man you lived with for twenty years is a monster, but he is.'

Fourteen

Frank met me at the door. I was still wearing my Little Black Dress from dinner hours earlier. Nonetheless, I slid down on to the floor and hugged him.

'What do we do now, Frank?' I said into his furry ear. 'My God, what do we tell Eric?'

Frank, expecting me to act the way I usually did when I was wearing something that attracted dog hair, pulled back and regarded me suspiciously.

At least it showed he had better instincts than I did.

Talk about a malfunctioning radar. I was suspicious and a little afraid of Pavlik, who was on the periphery of my life. Ted, on the other hand, had *been* my life for a lot of years. And he was a murderer. And a thief.

How do you live with someone for twenty years and not see it? Shouldn't I have turned suddenly and caught him with an evil glimmer in his eyes? Shouldn't he have kicked a cat? Stiffed a waitress? Something?

But maybe Ted had just snapped. 'Good timing for that,' I said aloud. 'If you're going to snap and kill someone, do it when they have half a million dollars lying around.'

I wondered when they would arrest him. The crime had taken place in Milwaukee, but Ted lived in Brookhills. Would Pavlik be there? Would he let me know? And when would I tell Eric? *How* would I tell Eric?

I glanced at my son's pictures on the fireplace mantle. I never considered myself much of a parent. I wasn't the Kool-Aid mom or even the cool mom. I was the mom who was feeling her way through, learning as she went.

The one thing I did know early on was that I would die to protect my son. Being a fairly self-centered person, that took a while to get used to. So did the realization that even so, I couldn't keep him entirely safe.

Especially if the evil had lived in our house.

'How do I tell Eric?' I asked Frank, who had given up and was now sitting next to me, both of our backs against the door.

Frank licked my nose.

I sniffed. Probably not the smartest thing, but the inhalation of sheepdog spit didn't seem like a big deal right now.

Eric was a five-hour drive away. It was one thirty in the morning. If I left now, I could be there before he woke up. Break the news to him in person, before he saw it on television or the newspaper.

How would he take it?

I was divorced from Ted and *I* was horrified by what Pavlik had told me. Add the fact that Eric was Ted's flesh and blood . . .

'Maybe I could tell Eric I had an affair and Ted isn't his father,' I said. 'That way he won't worry he has evil genes.' Frank swiveled his head around to give me a look of canine disdain.

'You're right,' I agreed. 'Layering on fictional trauma on top of real trauma probably won't help matters. What if I—'

My purse, tucked between Frank and me, beeped.

Frank and I looked at it. 'You answer it,' I said.

He cocked his head.

No help forthcoming from Frank, I dug the purse out from between us and then the cellphone from within the purse. 'Call from Eric' the screen said.

As I went to open it, the ringing stopped. A reprieve for now, but I certainly wouldn't have time to drive up to Minneapolis before he tried again.

Eric was worried and I needed to call him back. First, though I'd figure out what I'd say. Maybe, I would—

Beep beep. 'Call from Eric' flashed in my hand.

Frank put his paw on my hand. 'I'm getting it,' I told him, and flipped the phone open.

Before I had a chance to say 'hello', I heard, 'Why do you have a cellphone if you never answer it?'

Fair enough question, but better saved for another day. 'I'm sorry,' I told him, 'but it stopped ringing before I could get to it. I was going to call you back.'

'I've been going crazy. Did you find Dad? Is he OK?'

'He's gone, Eric.'

'Gone?' It was almost a sob.

Geez, what an idiot I was. 'No, no. I mean, he's fine, as far as I know. It's just—'

An explosive sigh of relief on the other end interrupted me. 'Thank God. I was afraid . . . well, you know.'

'I do,' I said gently. 'I was worried about the same thing.'

'So you said he's gone. Where?'

'I don't know. The sheriff's department is looking for him.'

'You called the police?' he asked sharply.

'No, but Pavlik arrived just after I did. He saw the e-mail, too.'

'Great.' Eric sounded more perturbed than worried now. 'Just what Dad needs is your boyfriend on his tail.'

I didn't say anything to that, but Eric kept right on going. 'Why did Dad run anyway? Now everyone will think he really did it.'

'Yes.'

He must have heard something in my voice. Or maybe a lack of something. 'You think he did it, too? How can you say that?'

Hearing Eric's raised voice, Frank sniffed at the phone.

'I don't know what else to believe,' I said. 'He transferred all the money out of their accounts.'

'Of course he did,' Eric said angrily. 'How else is he going to live on the lam. Even if he went up to—'

He stopped.

'Up where?' I asked.

'I was thinking Canada, like that Lawrencia Bembenek chick did, but he'd need a passport now, right?'

It was true that if you drove northwest, Thunder Bay, Ontario, was only about a ten-hour drive. Canada was even closer if you went east via Detroit. Either way, though, Eric was right, Ted would need a passport.

'He has a passport,' I said. 'He and Rachel went to Dubai on their honeymoon. But I assume the police will put out some sort of alert at the border.'

'Maybe he already made it across.' Eric sounded hopeful.

Me, I was doubtful. 'Maybe. If he didn't hit traffic in Chicago and drove around the lake and up to Detroit, it would take him about six, six and a half hours to get to Windsor.'

'So if he left just after he sent the e-mail, he could already be there.'

'He could.' I didn't add that it would have taken Ted at least a little time to transfer the money to somewhere he'd be able to pick it up. I also didn't say it totaled a half million dollars. I doubted the authorities would release the amount, so I thought I was safe in withholding the information.

'What car did he take?'

'The Miata, I think.' I said, a little surprised at the question.

'That was stupid. The Saab gets better gas mileage.'

'True.' Then there was Rachel's Escalade, which was still missing. If Ted had killed Rachel, he'd also hidden the SUV somewhere.

When Eric didn't say anything, I asked. 'Are you OK, kiddo?' It was a stupid question, but I didn't know what else to say.

'Yeah, I'm OK. Just thinking.' He cleared his throat. 'Listen, Mom, it's awful late and I have two exams tomorrow.'

'You go to bed,' I said, relieved to have the conversation over. 'I'll call you when I hear something.'

'Or text,' Eric suggested. 'I can pick up a text in class.'

My journalism professor would roll over in his grave. Assuming he was dead. 'Gotcha. It's going to be all right, Eric.'

'I know it is, Mom,' he said.

We were both quiet.

'Dad didn't kill her,' Eric said after a moment. 'You know that, right?' He sounded more like the parent than the kid.

'I know,' I said, and hung up. Then I patted Frank on the

head. 'If I'm willing to die to protect him, I should also be willing to lie, right?'

Frank shook his head, stood up and padded off to bed.

I was reminded that I hadn't taken Frank out the night before, when he woke me at five a.m. This normally wouldn't be a hardship, but Wednesday was the one day that I could sleep in late. I worked ten a.m. to closing.

I'd had one of those 'it was just a dream' moments when I awakened, only to realize it wasn't. Once awake, I couldn't get back to sleep. So what does one do at five a.m., when you need to knock the cobwebs out?

You take your big ol' sheepdog for a run.

It had been a while since Frank and I had jogged together, so I wasn't sure how either of us would fare. To my surprise, it was like riding a bike. You don't forget. Frank remembered to drag me and I remembered to hang on to the leash.

All told, we did about two miles and I was feeling pretty virtuous by the time I'd showered and arrived at Uncommon Grounds. Not good, you understand. Virtuous.

I was working with Amy, who gave me a sympathetic hug when I came in. The fact I'd missed the commuter hours between six thirty and eight thirty meant I was spared the line out the door, each person with a different version of the news reports I'd been avoiding.

What I couldn't avoid, though, were the tennis moms. We had two tables of them. One tableful was wearing identical turquoise tops and black skirts. The others sported black and white – two women in black skirts and white tops, one in a white skirt and black top, and one in a white golf shirt with black shorts.

What this all said to the discerning Brookhills observer was that the players at table A (matching turquoise and black) were seasoned veterans of both tennis and tennis fashion and those at table B (black and white) were newbies. Essentially, the elite and the townies.

Brookhills, though, was nothing if not upwardly mobile. By next year, townie table B would be flaunting their matching Sport à la mode outfits and looking down their rackets at the new newbies.

I love America.

Seated at table A was Sophie, who was more tennis grandma than mom. When I saw her trying to catch my eye, I signaled her over.

'I don't mean to pry,' she said, 'but they said on the news that the police are looking for Ted. Are you all right?' Even Sophie couldn't quite keep a straight face on the 'pry' issue, but something about her smile looked odd.

'Did you get Botoxed?' I asked.

She glanced around furtively and leaned across the counter to whisper. 'Vickie had a Botox party last night and I got a free trial. Don't you think it's frickin' amazing? Look.' She ran her finger up and down her forehead just above her nose. 'The vertical wrinkle is gone.'

She had her eyes wide open and was holding her eyebrows aloft. The wrinkle was still there, but it was frozen, like a crevice in a glacier.

I glanced over at the A table, wondering which Brookhills Barbie was Vickie. All the ladies were staring back at me. In fact, both tables had been watching me since I'd latte'd and cappuccino'd them.

I knew what they wanted. Information. And they wouldn't give up until they got it. In Sophie, I had a friend who would relay the information both kindly and dependably. The next best thing to appearing on *Larry King Live*.

I smiled back at Sophie. 'You look wonderful, Sophie. Ten years younger.'

She seemed a little disappointed. I guess ten years would still put her at seventy and she was hoping for more than that. Still, Sophie had other things on her mind than her forehead.

'Maggy, what was that dang man thinking? They're saying he killed Rachel, stole her money and then ran.'

'I know.'

Her mouth tightened. 'You think he did it.' The voice was Sophie's, but the accusatory tone sounded just like Eric.

I opened my mouth to answer, without the slightest idea

what I was going to say. Happily, I was interrupted by the sleigh bells on the door.

When I looked up gratefully, I saw Stephen Slattery. Which made me even more grateful.

Sophie gave Stephen a sly smile, before turning back to me. 'I'll let you take care of your customer,' she said with an attempt at a wink.

As she returned to the table, she gave Stephen the once-over. He stepped up to the counter, pulling on his collar. 'I guess I know what women feel like when they pass a construction site,' he said.

'You should feel complimented,' I said. 'Sophie doesn't ogle just anyone.'

He gave me a shadow of a grin. 'I'm sorry if I caused you trouble last night. I understand you were there when the sheriff arrived at Rachel's house.'

I noticed it was no longer Ted and Rachel's house. Not that I could blame him.

'I was,' I said. 'But that certainly wasn't your fault. I should have been smart and done what you did when you saw the e-mail: call the sheriff instead of checking on Ted myself.'

Stephen stared at me for a long moment. 'You can't spend twenty years with someone and not care about them. Even after they betray you.'

'Betray,' I said. 'That's an awfully mild word for every-thing Ted has done. The cheating was nothing.'

'So you believe he killed Rachel now?'

Why did everyone keep asking me that? Why did it matter what I thought? 'I don't know what else to believe. Rachel was murdered and dumped into Lake Michigan. The money is gone and so is Ted.'

'So you know about the money?'

'I do. Half a million dollars could take him a long way.'

'Half a million is hardly worth killing for. It's a drop in the bucket these days.'

Spoken like a member of the A table. 'Sounds like your bucket is a whole lot bigger than mine.'

Stephen looked startled. 'I'm sorry. I sounded like my

mother there. The thing is that Rachel's trust fund is worth millions.'

'Millions? As in more than one or two?' I asked, leaning closer so no one else could hear. 'Did Ted get that, too?'

'My mother has the trust funds tied up so tight, even we can't get to the money without jumping through her hoops. She's made *damn* sure a spouse can never touch it. That's why Rachel had Ted sign a prenuptial agreement. Slattery money passes only to Slatterys. And, of course, Slattery heirs.'

'Now that Rachel is dead, who—' My question was interrupted by the beeping of my cellphone, which I had tucked under the counter in case Eric called. As I picked it up, it registered that a text message had been left.

I flipped the phone open. The message read: 'could dad be in lake teree'.

'Have you ever heard of Lake Teree?' I asked Stephen.

He craned his neck to see what I was talking about. 'Lake Teree?' He gave it a French pronunciation. 'I've never heard of it.'

'Me neither.'

Stephen took a step back from the counter. 'Listen, I need to leave. I just wanted to make sure you're all right.'

'Sure. Thanks,' I said absently, still studying the message. By the time I looked up, Stephen was gone.

That was quick. All of a sudden, I was starting to get weird vibes from Stephen. He had seemed like a regular guy, even in his fancy office. Today, though . . . he seemed more like a Slattery. Of *The* Slatterys. And why had he practically run out of the store just now?

I'd give that more thought, but first I wanted to get back to Eric. 'Where?' I texted.

I was waiting for the answering message when Sarah came in. She was flashing a couple of tickets.

'Hey,' she said. 'I have two tickets for tonight's Twilight Tour downtown. Want to go?'

'You enjoyed it so much the other night that you bought tickets for everyone?' I asked, taking the tickets. 'Who would I go with?'

'Me, you idiot.' She pulled them out of my hand. 'Saturday night's tour was cancelled.'

That explained why I'd seen Sarah and her Firebird heading home that afternoon, instead of toward downtown. I hadn't given it much thought in all my pre-Pavlik excitement.

'I don't know. I might not be good company. Besides –' I held up the phone – 'I'm waiting for a text from Eric.'

'So?' Sarah shrugged. 'Believe it or not, Maggy, those things are portable. You can walk with them. You can even drive.'

Sarcasm, I didn't need. Or maybe I did. I preferred it to her Barbie moments. 'I have to work until six,' I said, pulling out the brochure she'd left with me on Saturday.

'The tour starts at seven,' Sarah said.

I was busy looking at the brochure. Not so much because I was interested, but because I wanted to fill my mind with anything but the ugly mess my life had become. As luck would have it, though, one of the buildings on the tour was the Hamilton.

'It goes to the Hamilton,' I murmured.

'Of course,' Sarah said. 'It's one of the oldest buildings in Milwaukee.'

The silent cellphone was on the counter. For all I knew, Eric had texted before he went into class. I could never keep his schedule straight and when I did think I had it, he changed it. Sarah was right. He could get hold of me, whether I was here or at home.

Or, even, on a tour of the last place Rachel was supposed to go.

Fifteen

We'd agreed that Sarah would pick me up and we'd drive downtown together. At six fifteen, I locked up and went out to the front parking lot.

The unseasonably warm weather of the past few days had taken a more seasonable turn. The temperature had dropped to about forty-five degrees, which wasn't all that bad except that when I'd left home it had been seventy. The light jacket I was wearing couldn't stand up to the chill in the air and the stiff breeze that had kicked up.

I could go back into Uncommon Grounds or climb into the Escape to keep warm, but that would be like surrendering. It was spring, damn it, it should act like it.

I hoped it was warmer downtown or I was going to turn into an icicle on the walking tour. Lake Michigan has a moderating effect on the temperature, making it cooler near the lake during the summer and warmer during the winter. In April, it was anybody's guess.

I pulled my hands up into my jacket sleeves to keep them warm. Stephen's quick visit this afternoon was still bothering me. He'd said he wanted to make sure I was all right, but he'd left so abruptly it made me wonder what had precipitated it.

We'd been talking about Rachel's trust fund. Did he think I was pumping him for information? Or that he'd said too much about 'the family business'? Maybe he even thought I was after *his* trust fund?

Nah. My jeans and Uncommon Grounds apron might scream many things about me, but 'gold-digger' wasn't one of them.

A movement to my left caught my attention. Thinking it

might be 'dumpster man', I cautiously peeked around the corner. False alarm. A squirrel was scaling the tree next to the back door.

I checked my watch. Six thirty. Sarah was late. We'd barely make it to the tour, even if she arrived right now. Even worse, I still hadn't heard back from Eric and I was beginning to worry. His classes must be over by now.

I stomped my feet on the asphalt to keep warm and tried to remember what I'd been thinking about when the squirrel distracted me.

Ah, yes. According to Stephen, Rachel had millions tied up in a trust fund, presumably from her parents or her maternal grandparents, the Whitakers. That was money Ted couldn't touch. So why would he kill her for half a million, when he could have stayed married to Rachel and reaped the benefits of all of it?

Maybe the murder was an accident. Ted really hadn't meant to kick her, smash in her face and toss her in the lake.

Yeah, that was it. An accident. Right.

So . . . maybe it had initially been an accident. Maybe she'd fallen. Or maybe he'd even lost his temper and shoved her during an argument and she'd hit her head. Then he panicked and tried to cover it up by making it seem like a mugging.

No. Ted wasn't exactly the sharpest drill in the office, but even he couldn't believe the police would buy that. Pregnant woman, kicked in the stomach, beaten in the face – it was a much more personal murder.

Personal: lover. Friend. Family.

Brother?

I shivered, but not because of the cold. Could I actually be considering Stephen a suspect? I'd much rather think that witch of a mother had killed Rachel.

But . . .

When Rachel had gone off and married Ted, she'd deserted the family business, leaving Stephen to fill the role of 'golden child'. When she gets pregnant, though, she decides to come back into the fold.

A grandchild would become the center of the Slattery universe. Rachel, back in the company business, could lower Stephen's worth in the eyes of their mother. Add a multi-million dollar trust fund that likely would go to Stephen as the sole Slattery heir when Rachel died, and what did you have?

A motive for murder. And a much better one than Ted had.

The ungodly sound of the Firebird's horn interrupted my thoughts. Sarah's passenger door just missed me as she reached across and slung it open. 'Get in, we're late.'

'Whose fault is that?' I asked as I slid in.

I barely had the door closed before Sarah took off. 'We'll meet the group at the Hamilton.'

Perfect, since the hotel was all I really cared about seeing anyway. I only had Roger Karsten's word that Rachel hadn't shown up there. And Roger's word was always question-able in my book.

Stephen said Rachel must have returned to his office later to retrieve the key cards. What if she hadn't? What if Stephen had killed her and planted the keys on her body to incriminate Ted?

Yikes. My head was spinning. Rachel told me her brother caught Ted and his lover 'in the act'. But maybe Stephen was the one acting here.

The lover, the calendar, the key cards – could that all have been Stephen's invention? Right down to the supposed 'matching' of key cards to calendars?

If so, Ted could be completely innocent in this.

There was that pesky half million dollars, of course. But who could really blame him for taking that? By this point, he had to wonder if he was being framed. Assuming he had no role in Rachel's death, the money was rightfully his anyway. Maybe the only thing he could think to do was take the money and run.

'What in the hell are you thinking about?'

Sarah's voice snapped me from my . . . well, 'reverie' sounded way too peaceful for what was bouncing around in my head. 'You haven't said a word for twenty minutes.'

'Twenty minutes? Are we almost there?' I looked around.

Indeed, we were passing Miller Park, which meant we'd be at the Hamilton in minutes. I checked my watch. Ten to seven, we might still make it.

'Sorry. I was just thinking about the tour.' I wasn't willing to share my theory with Sarah yet. In fact, I wasn't willing to share it with anyone. For now.

We were a little late, but our tour group was still standing in front of the Hamilton. It seemed our fellow tour members were members of the Red Hat Society, a social group of older women who choose red hats and socialization over orthopedic shoes and loneliness. I knew about them because Sophie Daystrom is an enthusiastic member of the Brookhills chapter.

In fact, Sophie herself wiggled fingers at me over the tour guide's head. She was wearing a red fedora. It looked like a dyed version of the gray one that Henry, her off-again, on-again squeeze wore. She and the other ladies also sported purple or lavender outfits.

Sarah was looking around. 'I guess Emma isn't leading this one.'

Good guess. The tour guide was eighty'ish, a wizened five foot two, and male.

'The owners are remodeling the front entrance hall,' he told us after he'd taken our tickets, 'so we'll have to enter through the loading dock.' He flashed an unnaturally white smile at Sophie. 'But I'll be more than happy to help anyone who needs –' he cupped his hands – 'a lift.'

Sophie giggled.

I felt giddy myself. The loading dock was just what I wanted to see. I'd feared I'd have to sneak away from the group to do it.

I'd been giving the Stephen-as-suspect scenario more thought. If he had waited at the Hamilton and killed Rachel when she arrived, Stephen still would have to get her body to the lake to dispose of it. But an accomplice – Roger Karsten, for instance – would make it ever so much simpler.

Rachel could have shown up right on time and found the two of them waiting for her. After they killed her, the loading dock would be the perfect place to trundle the body to a vehicle without anyone seeing it.

There was the question of why Roger would get involved, of course. Maybe something to do with kickbacks of some kind. An inspector who 'found' something could cost a seller a lot of money. And save a buyer a bundle.

I was liking my theory more and more. And being able to include that sleaze Roger Karsten? Priceless.

Sophie dropped back to join me as we rounded the corner of the building.

'I think he likes me,' she whispered, nodding toward the back of the guide. 'I could get lucky tonight.'

'Lucky?' I was so distracted I tripped over a trash can, sending it toppling. A rat scurried out from behind me to investigate a tantalizing tangle of discarded pink coat and shabby brocade fabric, no doubt from the remodeling. The fabric might have graced the entrance hall of the Hamilton for decades, but now it lay beneath the remains of a half-eaten hamburger and a slice of pepperoni pizza covered in fine white fuzz. Trash à la mold – who could resist? Not the rat, by the looks of it.

Sophie put out her hand to keep me from falling into the smorgasbord. 'You bet your butt,' she said. 'I haven't eaten yet.' She kicked in the direction of the rodent.

'Don't incite the rats,' I scolded. 'Are you talking about a dinner invitation?'

Sophie shrugged. 'If that's what you people call it.'

I was afraid to ask for clarification.

'That was a mouse,' Sarah's voice said in my ear. For once she was a welcome distraction.

Sophie just kept talking. 'I was brought up on a farm, you know. With the animals and all, things were different there.'

I was completely confused. I turned to Sarah. 'Mouse?'

'Mouse,' she confirmed. 'What was different, Sophie?'

Nooooo.

'Meals,' Sophie said, falling in step with her. 'We had our big meal at noon and called it dinner. Our evening meal was supper and . . .'

Breathing a sigh of relief, I caught up to the tour guide, who was starting up the steps of the loading dock. 'Excuse me, but is the Hamilton completely empty now?'

The guide's pale blue eyes brightened as he caught sight of me. 'It is, with the exception of the construction workers in the lobby area. We're lucky they're allowing us in to see the place before further renovation takes place.'

As he put his key into the lock of what resembled a giant steel garage door, I glanced around. I wasn't sure what I thought I'd see. Signs of a vehicle being parked there? There probably had been thousands of vehicles in and out every year for all the years the Hamilton had been there. How exactly did I figure out whether any of them had been made by the vehicle Stephen had used, perhaps Rachel's own Escalade?

As for signs of 'disturbance' in the accumulated grime – something a TV investigator would take note of – well, dirt is dirt. At least to me. I've spent years trying to ignore it, in fact.

The old tour guide leaned down to grasp the handle in order to roll up the door. I went to help but he waved me off. 'This is how I get my exercise,' he said, easily lifting it. 'Next tour I use my left arm. That way I balance.'

I liked this guy. 'So do you come here a lot?'

He gave me a sideways grin as he waved the Red Hats through the entrance. 'You use that line on all the old guys?'

I laughed. 'No, just the ones who hold the Red Hat Ladies in thrall.' I nodded toward a gaggle of them who were glancing toward us while trying to look like they weren't.

'Red Hots, I call them,' he said. 'They're great gals. They keep me young, just like they're doing for themselves – going out on the town, having Botox parties and all.'

Startled, I glanced over to where Sophie had joined her friends. Sure enough, there wasn't an eyebrow moving in the bunch.

'They invited me to one of them last year,' our guide continued, shaking his head. 'Hurt like hell.'

'What did you have done?' Sarah had come up behind me.

'Crows feet,' he said. 'Helped for a while, but then it

went back to normal. Collagen in the lips lasted longer.'
He pursed his lips.

'You, you . . .' I started.

'Hell, yes. Even let 'em do make-up on me. We had a
high time.' With that, he turned to the group. Sarah and I
looked at each other.

'Good to see you again, ladies.' He gave a little bow. The
ladies twittered, while he turned to us. 'And to our newcomers,
welcome.'

Sophie turned to the Red Hat next to her. 'I know them.
Her husband –' she pointed at me – 'is wanted for murder.'

The ladies gasped, but more in delight than horror. I had
a feeling I was going to be invited to the next Botox party.

Our tour guide, on the other hand, didn't skip a beat.
'My name is Beaumont Hertel and I'll be your guide for
our excursion through the colorful history of the Hamilton
and the rest of the buildings on our tour.'

'The Hamilton was built in 1914 . . .' As he spoke he led
us through a less than impressive catacomb of hallways.
We were in the basement, after all.

'Hope he takes us above ground,' Sarah muttered. 'Fat
chance of condos being built down here.'

'So the building *is* being made into condos?' I asked.
'Rachel told me the Slatterys were planning to turn it into
a hotel.'

'From what I hear, there are two buyers looking at it.
The Slatterys and LongShore, a condo developer. I'm rooting
for the condos.'

'You handle LongShore's sales,' I guessed.

'You betcha. And in a building like this with city and
lake views, the units will be going for four-fifty on up, and
I do mean up. The upper floors will be a million or more.'

'Then my only hope *would* be a condo in the basement,'
I muttered, glancing around.

I didn't know if Rachel had been there, much less where
she would have gone if she was. As I opened my mouth to
ask Sarah what she thought a potential buyer would be
looking at, we emerged into a cavernous room.

'The Hamilton stands on six thousand wooden pilings,'

our guide announced. 'This was necessary, because, as you'll see by looking down, the hotel is built on an underground lake.'

The ladies edged over to the railing, peered down and gasped. Since they'd obviously done this tour before, I thought it was a bit of overacting for our benefit. Nonetheless, I went over to look. Sure enough, there were thick wooden poles – more like tree trunks, really – extending down into the murky water.

'The level of the water is carefully monitored,' Beaumont went on, 'because if the submerged pilings are exposed, they'll begin to rot.'

'Tell them the story, Beaumont. Tell them the story,' Sophie begged. She must have been on her best behavior for our guide. I hadn't heard a single 'swear' out of her since we'd arrived.

'It's an urban legend,' he warned, turning to Sarah and me. 'I have to tell you that by way of disclaimer.'

'Which means it's true and they won't let you say it,' one of Beaumont's Red Hots teased.

Beaumont just tipped his head. '*Legend* –' he emphasized the word – 'has it that one day 132 construction workers and engineers worked on this building.' He let it hang there dramatically. 'But only 131 left, at least by the door.'

Sarah snorted. 'It's not unusual for someone to be killed during the construction of a building this size. Especially back then.'

'You're quite right,' Beaumont said. 'In fact, this building is unusual in that no one died during its construction.'

'But you just said that one person did.' I dug out my cellphone. Still nothing from Eric.

'No, I said that one person never came out, at least through the door.'

Sarah rolled her eyes. 'Then how did he come out?'

Beaumont shrugged. 'We don't know. He just disappeared one morning.'

'They never found him?' I asked, knowing full well I was playing into his hands.

'They found him, all right,' Sophie said in a mysterious voice. 'But it's where they found him that's interesting.'

'Lake Michigan,' a Red Hot in a purple pantsuit piped up.

Sophie threw her a dirty look. 'Be quiet, Lady Vickie. I'm telling it.'

Ahh, Vickie. The Botox Party lady.

'Then tell it,' Sarah snapped impatiently. She was still anxious to get to the penthouse units.

'She frickin' ruined it.' Sophie said, forgetting to censor herself.

'Tell it!' Sarah demanded again.

'Fine. The man's body was found a month later in Lake Michigan,' Sophie said sullenly.

'How can that be?' It was another Red Hot lady, trying to smooth things over and give Sophie a chance to go for the dramatic finish. 'We're more than six blocks away from the lake.'

I was looking over the railing into the dark water below.

'The underground lake is connected to Lake Michigan,' I said, turning to Sarah. 'She went into the water here in the basement and her body found its way into Lake Michigan.'

'He,' Sarah automatically corrected. 'She –' Sarah pointed to Sophie – 'said it was a man who went missing.'

Then, as my meaning sunk in, Sarah just stared at me.

Sixteen

'That has to be the way it happened,' I said. Sarah and I were climbing down the loading dock steps. We'd left the tour early and I'd been filling her in on my theory. Knowing everything I knew, or thought I knew, I couldn't just tag along with Beaumont and the Red Hots. I had to do something.

I just had to figure out what that was.

'It's possible, I suppose,' Sarah said. She was still sulking about my making her leave before we could see the upper floors of the Hamilton. 'But why are you so sure that Stephen did it? Couldn't your beloved ex have murdered Rachel in the same way you think Stephen did?'

'He could have,' I admitted. 'But if you think about it, everything starts with Stephen. Stephen is the one who "caught" Ted cheating and can read the hotel key cards. He also has the most to gain from Rachel's death and the most to lose by the birth of Rachel's child.'

I pulled out my cellphone and looked at it, before dropping it back in my bag. Still nothing from Eric.

Where was he? Lake Teree? Maybe Sarah, with all her real-estate dealings, would know where that was. 'Have you ever heard of Lake Teree? I showed her Eric's text message.

'No,' she said, 'not around here. You sure it's not "terra", like "terra firma"?'

'Why? Is there a Lake Terra?'

'No, just asking.'

She was a big help. 'I'm going to text Eric again.'

I punched in: 'What is'. When I got to 'teree', I looked down to make sure the phone was divining the letters correctly. Staring up at me was not 'teree', but 'verd'. When I added an 'e', the readout changed to 'teree'.

'Verde,' I said out loud. 'Lake Verde.'

'Lake Verde? That's up north,' Sarah said. 'I thought you said "Teree".'

'That's what the phone said.' I showed it to her. 'See when you text message "verde" the predictive function gets to the last "e" and then guesses "teree", whatever the hell that is, rather than "verde".'

'Verde is Spanish for green,' Sarah said. 'Maybe the phone doesn't recognize foreign words.'

'Maybe not, but *I* recognize it,' I said. 'Lake Verde is where Ted's family cabin is.'

'You think he went there?'

'I *know* he went there.' And I was an idiot for not thinking of it earlier. If Ted was in trouble, he would run home. Given that his mom was in Paris or wherever, the fishing cabin on Lake Verde was the closest thing to home. 'But that's the least of my worries.'

'Finding your ex-husband, who you believe has been falsely accused of murder is the least of your worries?' Sarah looked surprised. 'What has happened to the Maggy Thorsen I know and love?'

'She's concerned about her son,' I said. 'Our cellphone company has spotty service in the northern part of the state.' I held up my cellphone. 'That's why I can't get hold of Eric. He's on his way to Lake Verde.'

While we were about a ninety-minute drive from Lake Verde, Eric's school was a good four or five hours away. Problem was, I didn't know when he had left. Hell, I didn't even know *if* he'd left. I texted him again with a 'where are you?' Still no reply.

'He'd better not have cut classes,' I muttered. 'He said he had exams today.'

'Unless he lied,' Sarah said. 'Then he could already be there.'

Sarah and I were on our way to Uncommon Grounds to pick up an old keychain I'd left in the office desk drawer.

On it were keys I didn't use any more. My old house with Ted, before I changed the locks. The house key a neighbor, long moved away, had given me to water her plants. Luggage keys for bags I could no longer lock. The usual. I was nearly sure that one of them was to the cabin in Lake Verde, a hundred miles due north of Brookhills.

'I sure hope not,' I said.

'Why?' Sarah glanced sideways at me. 'If you don't think Ted is a homicidal maniac, why are you worried?'

'Because I think Stephen Slattery *is* a homicidal maniac and he was looking over my shoulder when Eric texted me.'

'But you didn't know what Lake Teree was. How would Stephen know?'

'Because he's probably a lot more technologically savvy than I am. I just tried his cell and he's not answering either.'

Not that I'd have known what to say if he had. *Excuse me, but did you kill your sister?*

Sarah swung the Firebird into the back parking lot of Uncommon Grounds. I got out of the car and ran to the back service door.

If my theory was right, Ted had been telling the truth all along. Sure, maybe he'd fallen in love with Rachel and left me, but he hadn't cheated on her. There also wasn't any reason to believe he had been cheating on me. Except with Rachel, of course. Strangely enough, I felt like she and I were comrades-in-arms in some way. Death and hindsight will do that, I guess.

What a nightmare these last few days must have been for Ted. Nobody believed him about anything. He'd been accused of being a cheater, a womanizer and a murderer. And he'd had nowhere to go.

Except Lake Verde.

Making my way through the dark service hall, I tripped over a bag of garbage, splitting it open and sending coffee grounds flying. Cursing my stupidity for having left it there in the first place, I let myself into Uncommon Grounds and went directly to the office.

I switched on the light and opened the desk drawer. Rifling through the pencils, pens, rubber bands and tiny bottles of Advil and Tylenol, I came up with a ring of old keys attached to a leather tag with a snap.

The tag snapped into a purse I no longer had, one that dated back to the early days of my marriage. I might not remember what each key was for, but I remembered every handbag I'd ever had.

The key for the cabin was on the ring, and wonder of wonders, efficiently marked with an 'LV'. It looked like Eric's printing, which would figure. He was the most organized member of the family. When he was five he alphabetized the contents of the refrigerator. *Sesame Street* had a lot to answer for.

Tucking the keys into my pocket, I grabbed a new black trash bag and went back into the service hallway. I didn't have time to do a good clean-up, but I stuffed the torn bag in the new one and lugged it out.

Letting the service door lock behind me, I lifted the key ring in one hand and the bag of garbage in the other to indicate to Sarah that I'd accomplished one mission and still had another one.

The box spring was still next to the dumpster. Friday was trash day and we'd see what they took then. I hoisted the bag into the dumpster, closed the gate and went back to Sarah's car.

'You had to take out the trash?' she asked mildly when I slid into the passenger seat. 'It couldn't have waited until we saved the world?'

It could have, of course, but . . . 'The bag broke and I couldn't leave a mess.'

Sarah pulled around the corner of the store to exit on to Brookhill Road. As she did, I saw a couple of people standing outside the dental clinic.

'Isn't the clinic usually open on Wednesday night?' I asked.

Sarah glanced at the clock on the dash. 'It's after eight. They're probably gone.'

'They should put up a sign then.' I pointed toward the man and woman standing outside. 'They look cold.'

The two were neatly but warmly dressed, like they were

going to a soccer game or football game, where they would be outside for a long period of time. The woman wasn't the same one I'd seen on Saturday, but she had that same fish out of water look.

The suburban poor, as Amy had suggested? Funny how I'd never noticed them until now.

Sarah pulled out on to Brookhill Road, heading east toward the interstate. She seemed to be puttering in comparison to her usual breakneck speed.

'Could you step on it? Like you said, Eric could be there already.'

'I've gotten caught at the speed trap on Brookhill twice already. I'm not getting another $250 ticket for you or anyone. Besides, why are you so sure that your son, who comes home only when he has to, is driving all the way from Minneapolis to Lake Verde?'

'Eric may not be good at visiting or even calling, but he is nearly compulsive about texting.'

'So?' Sarah turned on to the ramp heading north and accelerated to her normal speed – ten miles per hour over the speed limit.

I settled in, feeling a little better now that we were on our way. 'So he didn't answer my original text. That means he's avoiding me because he doesn't want me to ask what he's doing.' E-mails and texting might be great for communication, but they were also wonderful for going incommunicado. You answered what you wanted and pretended you didn't receive the rest. I was a great pretender.

'Besides,' I continued, 'he thinks I believe Ted killed Rachel.'

'Do you?'

'No.'

Sarah looked at me.

'Fine. Maybe I did. But the evidence seemed—'

'Enough to convince you that your son's father was a murderer.' She shrugged. 'You can understand why Eric took the opposite view.'

I could. And I did. 'I think I was so hurt, thinking that

Ted had cheated on me again, that it was easier to believe he was evil than . . .'

'That he had never loved you.'

I glanced over at Sarah, startled. Getting this kind of insight from her was like seeing Attila the Hun turn into the Dalai Lama before your eyes. 'That's very, very . . .'

'What?' she snapped.

I searched for a word that wouldn't set her off. 'Perceptive,' I settled on.

She seemed mollified. 'I am perceptive,' she said, sitting a little higher in her bucket seat. 'No one gives me credit.'

'I'm sorry.'

There was a silence and then Sarah said, 'So you think Eric went to Lake Verde to help Ted?'

'That's my best guess.' I was thinking back on my conversation with Eric last night. 'He started to tell me something and then stopped. I think he was going to say that Ted probably went to the lake cottage, but then thought better of it. He likely assumed I'd tell Pavlik.'

'Fat chance of that,' Sarah grumbled. 'That would mean you actually trusted the man.' She slammed on her brakes to let a blue sports car she'd cut off in the first place back into the lane. 'Idiot,' she yelled.

'Want me to open the window so she can hear you?' I said, rubbing my ear.

'Not necessary. My voice carries.'

Amen to that. 'I don't think it's a matter of trust,' I said as the other driver tapped her brakes to get Sarah off her butt. It didn't work. 'I just don't want to be wrong again. I don't want to feel stupid.'

'You need to trust Pavlik with those feelings.'

'What are you doing, writing fortune cookies in your spare time?'

Sarah flushed. 'Emma dragged me to a yoga class.'

My mouth dropped open.

Sarah glanced over and shrugged. 'We meditate.'

I might be able to cope with the possibility Ted had been framed, but the thought of Sarah meditating? It would have to wait for another day.

Sarah changed the subject. 'Why didn't you think of Lake Verde in the first place?'

'I put it out of my head years ago. I hated that cabin. Ted took me there when we were dating, but I refused to go again.'

'Rats?' Sarah guessed.

'I thought so, but they might have been mice. They looked just like that mouse tonight. Either way, the cabin was dark, it was dirty and there were things living there that didn't belong there.'

'That's probably not the way they looked at it. And it was a rat, by the way.'

'In the cabin? How would you know?'

'At the Hamilton. I just didn't want you to freak.'

'I didn't freak. I was merely being prudent.'

'Sure,' Sarah said. 'So if you never go to the cabin, how does Eric know about it?'

'He and Ted went there to fish every summer when Eric was younger,' I said. 'It was Ted's father's favorite place. I don't think anyone has been up there since he died.'

Sarah changed lanes to pass a semi-trailer. 'If Eric didn't want you to know that he thought Ted was at the cabin, why did he text you about Lake Verde?'

I'd been thinking about that. 'Eric has a good head on his shoulders. Maybe he was scared of going up there alone, without anyone knowing where he was.'

One thing I'd stressed with Eric when he went away to school was that I needed to know when he left the Cities. Each year it seemed like more students disappeared from universities around the country. Some turned up alive, some dead. Others were just never heard from again. 'He could have gotten lost or hurt on the way. I think he showed good judgment.'

'True,' Sarah said. 'But maybe he's also not as sure of Ted as he wants you to think.'

'Yeah, there's that, too.'

'So are we showing "good judgment"?' Sarah asked after a moment.

We exchanged looks. Then I got out the cellphone and called Pavlik.

Two dropped calls and a bad connection later, I'd filled the sheriff in. As I expected, Pavlik dismissed my theory on Stephen or at least seemed to. He also wasn't all that happy I was on my way to Lake Verde.

'Did you even consider telling me about the lake property?' he asked. He'd just finished reaming someone on the other end for not finding the cabin in their background check of Ted.

'I'd forgotten about it,' I said, honestly. 'And before you send someone to the guillotine, the cabin belongs to Ted's mother, not to Ted.'

I pointed and Sarah took a right on to a single lane asphalt road.

'Doesn't matter,' he grumbled. 'We should have found it.'

I let that go, since I was glad he'd stopped yelling at *me*.

'It sounds like the cabin is pretty far off the beaten track,' Pavlik said. 'I'll head up, but we'll also contact law enforcement up there. How far away are you?'

Thanks to Sarah generally knowing how to get to Lake Verde and my loathing the cabin enough to remember every turn that took me away from civilization, we had navigated our way with little problem.

'Close,' I said.

'How close?'

'Umm . . .'

'Pulling up the driveway close,' Sarah said loudly.

'You're there?' Pavlik thundered. 'Think you could have waited any longer to call me?'

'Thanks,' I said to Sarah sourly.

To Pavlik I said, 'We kept losing cell service. We're on a country lane leading to the lake. We're still a few miles away.'

'Define "few",' Sarah muttered.

'Is that Sarah with you?'

'Yes.'

Sarah gave me a dark look.

'Good,' Pavlik said. 'At least she has some common sense. If you're right and Stephen Slattery is involved and knows Thorsen is in Lake Verde, he could go looking for him. Can I trust you not to go into the cabin?'

It was the first inkling I'd gotten that he'd actually been listening when I told him my theory about Stephen.

'Don't worry,' I said. 'I'll be careful. Is there anything else I should know?'

'Yes. You are not a cop. Stay out of the cabin.' He was talking in clipped sentences. He meant business. I didn't care.

'Gotcha,' I said.

The sound on the other end might have been a growl.

'I think I'm losing service again,' I said. We were passing through a hilly area of glacial formations. Every time we went up moraine and down kettle, the volume of Pavlik's voice followed suit.

'Results . . . did she say . . .'

'You're cutting out,' I said loudly into the phone.

We came up a rise and I heard, '. . . Rachel never told you she was pregnant?'

'The first I heard of it was when you said something at Ted's house,' I said.

We were heading down the other side of the rise, and static kicked up again. Then, '. . . autopsy showed . . . not pregnant . . .'

'What?' I yelled.

'Damn!' Sarah said, rubbing her ear. 'And you say I'm loud?'

I didn't answer. I was looking at the useless phone. No bars indicating service. Not one.

'I assume you lost him?' Sarah asked.

I turned to Sarah. 'Yup, he's gone. Thing is, I think Pavlik was saying that Rachel wasn't pregnant when they found her.'

'She miscarried? Why wouldn't she tell anyone?' She flicked on her turn signal and changed lanes to pass another truck.

'I don't know. Maybe she couldn't face people's reactions. That mother of hers is no prize and she was apparently thrilled Rachel was pregnant. If Rachel lost the baby, I can just see her mother blaming Rachel for it.'

'C'mon,' Sarah said, slowing on a blind curve. 'I never had one of the little buggers myself, but even I know a miscarriage isn't anyone's fault.'

I looked sideways at her. 'You *have* met Mrs Slattery, right?'

'Unfortunately, yes,' Sarah said. 'She's such a bitch I was tempted to drop the Slatterys as clients.'

'What changed your mind?'

Sarah gave a horsey laugh. 'Commissions. Do you know what six percent comes out to when you're buying and selling hotels? Besides, Stephen started to get involved and took over the real-estate dealings. He's a dream to deal with.'

More like a nightmare, if you were Rachel. 'If Rachel had told Stephen about the miscarriage, she might still be alive.'

'*If* you're right about him.'

I had to be right. Because if I was wrong, the only other solution was that Ted had killed Rachel.

And if that were true, Eric was driving straight into the arms of his loving, albeit murderous, father.

The property was dark as we drove up the gravel drive. The only reason I knew the cabin was there was that it stood in a clearing, a square one story with a triangle top, silhouetted against the reflection of the moon on the lake beyond it.

I didn't say it wasn't beautiful; I said it had rats. Not to mention the half-centipede I'd found in my Diet Coke glass our second day there.

'There's the Miata,' I said, pointing to the little blue car tucked into the trees next to the drive. 'That means Ted is here, but there's no sign of Eric's van, thank God.'

'Or Slattery?' Sarah asked, pulling to a stop just behind the Miata.

'Nope.' I was starting to relax. Maybe this was all going to work out. I'd go in and tell Ted I suspected he'd been framed. Then I'd talk him into surrendering to Pavlik. We could even have coffee while we waited for the sheriff.

Pleased with myself, I got out of the car. When I closed the door the dome light went out, leaving me in the dark. 'I can't see a thing out here. A little ambient city light would be nice.'

'But then you can't see the stars,' Sarah said, opening her door to step out. 'I've never seen so many.'

As she looked skyward, I grabbed her shoulder. 'Don't go all Brookhills Barbie on me here. I need the old Sarah. The one who thinks stargazing, not to mention tennis, is a waste of time.'

'I just said there were a lot of them,' she muttered defensively. 'Not that I *liked* them.'

'That's my girl.' I hesitated. 'Is that a light?' I was pointing toward the cabin, a good fifty yards away.

Even as I spoke, a light arced across the front of the cabin. Headlights of a car, coming up the driveway behind us. The faint glow in the house went out. Ted must have seen the light.

'It's Eric,' I whispered to Sarah. It wasn't so much the shape of the vehicle coming up the rutted drive, but the sound. Eric was driving my old minivan and I knew every rattle and groan of the pathetic old thing.

I wanted to reason with Ted without our son there. Eric didn't know the details and I preferred it stayed that way.

'Stop Eric and wait for the police,' I hissed. 'I'm going up to the cabin to talk to Ted.'

'Just how am I going to stop Eric?'

'He has headlights. Stand in the middle of the driveway and wave.'

Sarah folded her arms. 'Are you crazy? I am not going to throw myself in front of a teenager in a minivan. Not for you, not for anybody.'

'Chicken.' I stepped out and waved. The minivan stopped in a spray of gravel.

'See?' I said over my shoulder to Sarah.

As I approached, I could hear muffled sounds from inside the van. I couldn't make out the words until Eric opened the driver's side door. The automatic windows had quit being automatic about a year ago.

'What are you doing here?' he demanded.

'It's good to see you, too, sweetie.' I leaned in to give him a hug. The 'sweetie' always made him roll his eyes, but the hug he took.

I stepped back to look at my son. In the dome light of the van, he could have been a young Ted. It was only when you studied Eric more closely that you saw that his eyes were more hazel than green and his hair was dark, instead of sandy brown.

'I'm here for the same reason you are,' I said. 'To look for your father.'

'Is Pavlik with you?' Eric looked around like he expected the sheriff to pop out from behind one of the trees. Eric liked Pavlik, but apparently drew the line at his arresting Ted.

'No, just Sarah.' I gestured toward Sarah, who was still standing safely on the shoulder of the drive.

I swallowed hard. There had been enough lies and half-truths in this family. 'I did call Pavlik. He's sending the local police.'

'Mom, why would you do—' Eric started, but I held up my hand.

'For your protection, Eric. I—'

Interrupting ran in the family. 'Dad would never hurt me.'

'It's not Dad I'm worried about.' I turned to Sarah, who had come over to join us. 'You two stay here and wait for the police. I'm going to see Ted.'

'I'm going with you.' Eric started to climb out of the driver's seat.

'No,' I said again. 'You need to pull the van behind the Firebird. Then wait for me here. I'll let you know when it's all right to come in.' Ted was still a suspect and if the police came in with guns, I didn't want Eric in the line of fire.

He tried to protest, but this time it was Sarah who interrupted. 'Listen to your mother,' she snapped.

Eric's face registered surprise. 'Yes, ma'am.'

I looked at Sarah with new respect. 'You're getting good at this mothering stuff.'

'Sam and Courtney are away visiting friends this week,' Sarah said. 'I need to keep my skills up. Stay sharp.'

'Sharpen away,' I said. Eric already was pulling the van over, so I started up the driveway, trying to be fast and quiet.

I didn't want to startle Ted. I didn't think there was anything more lethal than a can opener and a fly rod inside, but I couldn't be sure. As I stepped on the first step leading up to the porch, though, the board creaked and a dog started to bark.

ChiChi, the chihuahua.

Best to identify myself. 'Ted?' I called. 'It's me, Maggy.'

I climbed the rest of the steps and peered between the slats of the shutters. All looked dark. ChiChi continued to bark, but no one was shooshing him.

Maybe he was the only one there. ChiChi and the rats.

I shuddered. It was dark, it was cold, and there were rats of both the canine and rodent variety inside. There might even be a human one.

I had my hand on the doorknob to try the door when I stopped.

Was this a good idea?

Eric was safe. Or as safe as anyone could be in Sarah's care. As for Ted, Pavlik was—

Crash.

The sound was followed by whimpering.

ChiChi? Maybe. But I also thought I heard something else. Groaning. And the groaning sounded familiar.

Just like I had known the sound of my old minivan coming up the gravel drive, I recognized the groan of my ex-husband. Ted could be in real trouble, injured or even dying.

Then again, I'd heard him sound just as pathetic when he had the sniffles.

The sound came again. Without thinking, I turned the knob. The door, damn it, swung open.

Seventeen

As I stepped in, I was greeted by darkness, a puddle of piddle and a chihuahua. Sort of took the edge off.

Another groan. It sounded like it came from the floor directly in front of me. As I carefully shuffled forward, my eyes started to become accustomed to the dark. It helped that moonlight was streaming through the windows at the back of the house where the kitchen was located.

I slid sideways along the wall next to the door until I found a light switch. A dusty gooseneck lamp in the corner flickered on.

Ted was on the floor, his mouth covered with a piece of duct tape and a chair tipped over next to him. Even I realized this meant he was not alone. Had Stephen come and gone, leaving Ted tied up? Or was he still there?

Ted's eyes were open and he was trying to say something, defeated by the duct tape. As I edged my way closer, I saw that his hands and legs also were bound with tape.

Along with cockroaches, duct tape could probably survive a nuclear winter. I pulled at the tape. It stretched a bit, but that was it. There was likely a knife in the kitchen, but God knew what else was in there. Maybe Stephen Slattery. Or rats.

Having sniffed at the fresh air outside and found it wanting, ChiChi came skittering back to see what I was doing. When he started to whine, I put my hand out and the little bugger tried to take a chunk out of my thumb.

'Bite the tape, you weenie, not me.' I slid him out the way.

'Are you OK?' I asked Ted as I fumbled at the duct tape. I planned to pull it off his mouth in one quick movement if I could ever find the end. Ted's eyes were panicky. He knew I was a 'take no hostages' Band-Aid kind of person.

As I got ready to yank, I heard ChiChi's toenails on the floor behind me. Turning to push him back again, I met beady eyes backed up by a long tail.

Rats. Or rat.

As I jumped up, ChiChi sprang out of the shadows barking. The rat turned tail and ran with the chihuahua in pursuit.

I stood for a second, letting my heart settle back down where it belonged. I'd seen enough rats today, between here and the Hamilton.

I stopped.

I was picturing the rat at the Hamilton when it had disappeared under the pile of garbage. The tomato sauce of pizza, accenting the quilted fabric underneath.

Pink quilted coat.

Or had it been a 'mauve' puffy jacket, as Amy put it?

The woman I'd seen going to the dental clinic the morning of Rachel's disappearance had been wearing a parka that looked a lot like the discarded one in the trash of the Hamilton.

Coincidence? Maybe. But . . .

I thought about the box spring stripped of its fabric and next to the dumpster. Caron said it had looked nearly brand new when she first saw it there. Who had ripped it and why?

Ted was banging on the floor, trying to get my attention. I leaned down and, in one swift movement, ripped the duct tape from his mouth.

The first sound out of it was a scream of pain. The second: 'She's here.'

'I know,' I said, and turned.

Eighteen

Emma Byrne. And she had a gun.

'Uh-oh.' Ted said from his position on the floor.

Emma stepped out of the kitchen where she must have hidden when she heard me come in. I held up my hands and started backing toward the door.

'Stop now,' Emma said. 'You don't want to get hurt.'

'It's a little late for "don't want to's", isn't it?' I asked, still backing.

Emma's blue eyes were glistening with tears. 'You don't understand. We didn't want any of this to happen. Rachel . . .'

Ted groaned. His lips looked like he'd been at Lady Vickie's Botox and Collagen Party.

'. . . she was the anointed one. Stephen barely registered on the Slattery scale. Things were better when Rachel left the company, but then she got pregnant and we knew it was all over. Eve would never let go of that baby. Nothing and nobody else would matter.'

'*If* Rachel was pregnant,' I said.

'What do you mean?'

'I mean, she sat in my living room and drank wine. Would she do that if she was pregnant?'

'You're lying.'

I stepped back toward the doorway keeping my hands still up. I was hoping Sarah and Eric would see me.

'Stop!' Emma waved the gun at me. I wasn't sure she could shoot it, but she sure was good at waving it.

'I'm unarmed,' I said. 'If you shoot me, it's murder. But then you've already committed murder.'

'That's not true.'

'I get that you were having an affair.' I gestured in a 'no-harm-no-foul' kind of way, as she bristled. 'I also understand that two people in an affair –' I looked down at Ted – 'could truly love each other. But what I don't understand is why you had to involve poor Ted here. Why frame him? The key cards, the calendars, the supposed affair – with you, in fact.'

Emma looked startled. 'People thought I was having an affair with Ted? Whoever said that?'

Good question. But remembering whether anyone had actually said it or it was just a figment of my fertile imagination would take more brain cells than I could muster right now.

'Why is it so far-fetched?' I asked. 'After all, you've known each other since dental school. Even I wondered.'

'Really?' Emma looked genuinely aghast. 'But that's ridiculous.'

'Yes. But I didn't realize it at the time.' I waited a beat, then added. 'And I'm betting you didn't either.'

She stared at me for what seemed like a minute, but was probably five seconds. Then she nodded. It might not have been outright acquiescence, but it was certainly acknowledgement.

I sensed an opportunity and ramped up the empathy. 'This isn't going to work. You know that, don't you?'

She didn't answer. She was staring at me again, like I could see right through her.

I wished I could, but having her think I could was almost as good. 'No one gets to live happily ever after, Emma.'

'Why not?' she whispered. 'All the songs and the movies tell us we can. They make us believe in fairy stories.' She gave an ironic little laugh.

The gun leveled up toward me. 'Why can't they just leave us alone? Why can't we just be happy?'

'Because you're not like "them",' I said. 'You can never live up to their standards.'

Emma was weakening, but I suspected she had reinforcements nearby. I just didn't know how nearby.

The nose of her gun dropped a bit and I started forward.

At the same time, a yellow blur came through the doorway. A tennis ball.

Leave it to Sarah. Too bad she hadn't taken up bowling.

ChiChi sprang after the tennis ball as it ricocheted off the wall and back toward Emma. Taking advantage of the diversion, I dove at her. We fell to the ground, Emma still holding the gun, me trying to keep it from pointing at me. As we struggled, a shadowy figure appeared over us.

'It's over,' a voice said.

I'd just gotten the upper hand on the gun, so I wasn't buying. Besides, in the last year or so, I'd become a huge proponent of the 'act quickly, apologize later' school of thought.

Wrenching the gun out of Emma's hand, I pointed it.

Nineteen

Rachel Slattery Thorsen shook her head at me. 'I really wanted to like you.' She, too, had a gun. Hers was bigger than mine.

And, despite what we tell men, size does matter.

I stood up, still keeping my gun trained on her. 'You liked me so much that you stole my husband and, when you tired of him, framed him for your murder?'

'Please. It's not that simple,' Rachel said. 'Now, put down your gun.'

'Why? You have one and I have one. You put yours down.' I hoped I sounded more confident than I felt.

'Good try. But I'm willing to bet you've never shot a gun. I have.' Rachel moved sideways so she was behind Ted and tipped the gun toward him. 'Put it down or I'll demonstrate.'

I set the gun down on the floor. Ted's eyeballs went back into their sockets.

Rachel smiled and kicked the gun toward the kitchen. She was wearing athletic gray sweats and tennies. Judging by the mud on her shoes, she'd been digging.

'Where are those great boots you had on the other day, Rachel?' I said. 'Oh, wait. You needed to put those on a homeless woman, beat her to death in my dumpster corral and dispose of her body at the Hamilton.'

I smiled sweetly at her. 'I forgot.'

'We did *not* kill her,' Emma said. 'Why do you keep saying that?' She'd gotten up and was now cowering behind Rachel. 'I found her dead. We only hit her in the face so no one could identify the body.'

'Right,' I said. 'So why was there so much blood on the box spring? You had to rip it off and dispose of it. What did you use to hit her? The paint cans?'

Emma turned to Rachel. 'Wait a second. She wasn't dead when you hit her?'

'You're the doctor,' Rachel said, stepping away from her. 'You said she died in your office, probably a cerebral hemorrhage after her boyfriend beat her up. You're the one who said we weren't hurting anyone.'

'*I* didn't hit her. You did.' Emma came around Rachel so she could confront her directly. 'Why didn't you tell me about the blood?'

'You might want to ask her about the whole pregnancy thing while you're at it,' I suggested mildly from the sidelines. Ted made an 'ummph' noise, so I nudged him gently with my toe. He shut up.

'Did you drink wine?' Emma asked Rachel indignantly. 'How could you do that to our baby?'

'First of all,' Rachel said, 'I pretended to take a sip. I did not drink. Second of all, *it's not your baby.*'

Rachel pointed the gun down at Ted. 'It's his.'

Ted cringed. At this point, I had little sympathy for him. Duct-taped or not, he wasn't being much help here. Even ChiChi had been more valuable. In fact, even the rat had been more useful.

Nonetheless, Ted was the father of my child.

'Why did you come up here to the cabin?' I asked Rachel to divert her. I was biding my time, hoping that Pavlik's cavalry would arrive.

'Ted had told me about this place. I thought it would be a good place to hide. Then he –' she nodded toward Ted – 'showed up.'

'Inconsiderate of him not to have called first,' I observed. 'It *is* his cabin, though.'

'His mother's cabin, you mean.'

'Just like everything you have is controlled by *your* mother,' Ted piped up indignantly from the floor. 'You have a lot of nerve talking about living off your family.'

'I worked,' Rachel said. 'I was a dental hygienist, for

God's sake. You know how many hours we spend on our feet. You know how many of us get carpal tunnel.'

'There's a difference between getting carpal tunnel because you need to and carpal tunnel because you want to,' I said. 'There's also a difference between earning a good, honest wage to live your life and doing the same to prove . . .' I stopped.

'To prove what?' Rachel demanded waving the gun.

I could see the growing fear in Ted's eyes and even ChiChi had stopped playing with the tennis ball. He was looking back and forth between Rachel and me.

'To prove what?' I said, echoing Rachel. 'That you're not your mother.' I waited three beats. 'Or is it your father that you don't want to be like?'

'Neither,' she snarled, advancing. Apparently I'd hit a nerve. 'My mother is a bitch and my father is a wimp. I am neither.' Each of the last three words was annunciated clearly, like she was affirming it to herself.

'And yet,' I said, fighting the urge to back up, 'you can't escape from either.'

'I *can*,' she screamed. 'I *have*.'

'But even now, not on your own dime. No, you escape from your mother by stealing *my* husband.' I could see Ted using his duct-taped hands and feet to propel himself slowly toward the door.

'Then you go and get pregnant,' I said, trying to keep Rachel's attention on me and off of Ted. 'That was the last thing you wanted, wasn't it?'

Her eyes were huge now. 'If I had a child, my mother would never let go of either of us. She would always have "a right" to my baby. I couldn't let that happen.'

A hostage to the Slattery fortune.

'You can't contemplate adoption or abortion, of course.' I lowered my voice and made it sing-song. 'After all, what would Mommy say—'

'He wouldn't have let me anyway.' She gestured with the gun toward Ted, who froze. 'You were married to him. He loves Eric. Do you honestly think he'd let me abort his baby?' She sounded ticked that Ted would even have a say in it.

'Why did you marry me?' Ted asked from the floor. 'If you love her –' he tipped his head toward Emma – 'why weren't you with her? Things could have stayed the same,' he said, almost to himself.

I knew he meant for us – him and me and Eric. And they could have. But maybe that wouldn't have been for the best.

I didn't say that, though. What I said instead, was: 'Rachel move in with another woman? Whatever would Mother say?'

'Shut up.' Rachel was moving toward me.

'Rachel isn't like that,' Emma protested.

'Really? You two have been lovers for years, right? Probably since Rachel worked for you.'

Emma nodded.

'So did she ever take you home? Introduce you to Mom and Dad?'

'No, but I understood that. She hasn't come out and neither have I. She couldn't—'

'And whose idea was it to stay . . .' I was searching for an alternative to the clichéd 'in the closet'.

'In the closet,' Ted suggested.

At least I'd been saved from saying it myself.

'We agreed,' Rachel said firmly. 'Both of us.'

'OK, so you weren't going to admit you were lovers. But you've known each other for years. Did you ever introduce her to your parents as your boss? Or your friend?'

'No, of course not,' Rachel said. 'There was never an opportun—'

'That's not true,' Emma interrupted. 'There were plenty of opportunities, but you always made me leave. Or hide.' She looked at Rachel, seeming genuinely puzzled. 'Why would you do that? They wouldn't know—'

'But they would,' I said. 'At least Rachel thought so. Right, Rachel?' I turned to her. 'You are so intimidated by your mother that you thought she would know Emma was gay just by looking at her.'

Emma laughed. 'That's ridiculous.' She turned to the other woman. 'Tell her.'

But Rachel didn't say anything.

Emma looked stunned. '*Tell* her,' she said again.

Rachel flushed and shook her head.

'Is that what you think?' Emma asked. 'That she has superpowers? Or maybe it's me. Maybe I just give off lesbian-vibes, huh?'

'That's not true,' Rachel protested, laying a hand on her arm. 'But my mother would have hated you. She would have known you make me happy and she would have destroyed it.'

Quick thinking on Rachel's part and it worked. Emma softened.

Time to try another tack.

'So suddenly you have the courage to leave,' I said. 'Why?'

'The baby.' Emma was back in the role of lover. 'We both wanted this baby, *our* baby –' she looked at Rachel, who this time didn't contradict her – 'to be free of the Slatterys.'

'How noble of you. But what about him?' I gestured at Ted, who had pretty much given up wiggling and was now watching us from his modified fetal position. 'First you take his child, then you steal his money,'

'*My* money,' Rachel interjected.

I ignored her. 'And, finally, you use Stephen to frame Ted for your "murder".'

I raised my hand for a high five. 'Now *that's* the kind of stand-up gals you are.'

Neither high-fived me back.

'Ted was cheating on me,' Rachel said. 'Stephen cared enough about me to warn me.'

'That gave you a great excuse to dump Ted, not to mention frame him. No one, not even Emma –' I nodded at her – 'who seems to have a conscience, could blame you.'

No response from Emma. I'd lost her.

'Did you think to ask Stephen who Ted was supposedly cheating with?' I asked Rachel. 'Because if you had, he'd have told you it was Emma.'

This time it was Rachel who turned on Emma. 'You had sex with Ted?'

'We were just friends,' Emma protested. 'We had sex once and that was way back when I still thought I was straight. In fact, he was engaged to . . .' She looked at me and slapped her mouth closed.

Then all three of us looked at Ted, helpless on the floor.

'You have *got* to be shitting me,' I said.

Ted said, 'Ummph,' and then shut his mouth.

Good move.

Still, I couldn't afford to lose my focus here. I needed to keep them talking. With any luck, the police would arrive. Or Sarah would toss another tennis ball in.

'So Stephen tells you he saw Ted and Emma together and you, knowing their past *dalliance* –' I threw Ted a dark look – 'purposely turned an innocent molehill into a sleazy mountain.'

Rachel didn't respond.

'Poor Stephen,' I continued. 'He didn't realize you were using him, any more than I did when you asked for my calendars so I would support your story. You and Emma just planned on disappearing, leaving Ted a suspect and Stephen and me with loads of questions, but no answers.

But then Emma called on your cell while we were in Stephen's office and suggested the perfect way to tie up all the loose ends. This "dead body" had just dropped into her hands. You blew off your appointment with Roger Karsten and went to help her.'

I turned to Emma. 'It was perfect. Rachel had started seeing you, both personally and professionally, when she worked for you. That meant that both she and the home-less woman were your patients. You could switch the dental X-rays and, presto, the dead woman is Rachel.

'After your call, Rachel stops at home to pick up some things – probably that lovely sweatsuit and a few more key cards – and then the two of you go to dispose of the body at the Hamilton, where it would eventually be found and believed to be Rachel. Only problem is, your dead body . . . does she have a name?'

'Gretchen,' Emma said quietly. 'Her name was Gretchen.'

'Yes, Gretchen. Well, Gretchen isn't dead. Rachel finds

this out when she goes to smash in her face and Gretchen bleeds all over the place. Rachel cleans up the box spring the best she can, stripping the bloody fabric and disposing of it. But she never bothered to tell you, did she?'

Emma shook her head.

'The pink parka was your mistake, you know.'

'Parka?' Emma echoed.

'Gretchen was wearing the parka when I saw her go into your office Saturday afternoon. When Sarah and I were at the Hamilton today, I saw the coat along with the brocade drapes you must have wrapped the body in. That's when I realized Emma was involved.' I cocked my head. 'Hear that siren? The police are here.'

In truth, I didn't hear a siren, but I did hear something else fast approaching. And it sounded familiar.

Crash.

The front end of the minivan joined us in the living room, coming to rest a foot from Ted's head.

I jumped Rachel, the greater of the two evils. As she and I fell to the floor, I saw Eric storming in from the kitchen.

Distracted, I let Rachel get the upper hand, pinning me down, my back to the ground. She straddled me and raised her weapon.

'I've got the other gun!' Eric yelled. 'You hurt my mom and I'll kill you.'

I had no doubt that my son would die to protect me. It went both ways.

As Rachel turned her gun toward Eric, I smacked her on the side of the head and did a stomach crunch that would have made any Brookhills Barbie proud. Lifting a little up and a lot sidewise, I managed to tip Rachel off me. Then I scrambled on to my knees, shoving my knuckles against her larynx, like I'd seen on TV.

'Drop the gun,' I said, 'or I will crush your windpipe.'

'My baby,' she cried, trying to bring her gun up at me.

'*My* baby.' I jerked my head toward Eric, 6'2" and with a gun in his hand.

Rachel dropped her gun.

Twenty

Sarah climbed out of the minivan and surveyed the scene. Rachel was still on the ground. I had her gun and Eric was holding his on Emma.

Sarah shook her head. 'You just can't stand it when I make new friends, can you?'

'You choose badly,' I said.

'Put down your weapons,' a voice boomed out. Suddenly we were surrounded by uniforms.

I looked at Eric. 'Slowly set it down on the floor so it doesn't go off accidentally,' I told him as I did the same.

He nodded, then we both raised our hands over our heads. 'We're the good guys,' I protested.

They ignored me. One officer was busy cutting Ted free of the tape around his feet and wrists.

'Are you Tor Thorsen?' the cop asked, as he helped Ted to his feet.

'Yes,' Ted said, wiping the blood off his lips. 'Thank God you're here. I—'

The cop slapped cuffs on him.

Ted's jaw dropped.

'You *are* officially a murder suspect,' I reminded him. 'It might take a while to sort out the fact the victim is still alive.'

'Who's Maggy Thorsen?' another voice boomed out.

I pointed to Sarah.

'Liar,' Sarah snapped.

'Fine.' I waved my hand, still held high. 'I'm Maggy Thorsen.'

Instead of his handcuffs, he pulled out his cellphone to call Pavlik. I almost asked for the cuffs.

*   *   *

Pavlik met us at the Lake Verde sheriff's office.

He talked to the deputies. He talked to Ted. He talked to Sarah. He even talked to Eric. *Then* he got to me.

'You didn't stay out of the cabin.'

'I heard Ted cry out. I knew he was in trouble and I had to help. Just like I'd help you or Eric. And just like Sarah and Eric helped me.'

'They did that. I don't think your minivan is going to make it.'

'I can stand that loss, though Eric might not agree. He's going to have to take the train or bus back to the Twin Cities.'

'I heard Ted say he was going to drive Eric up. Sounded like he wanted some father/son bonding time.'

'Ted's a good father. Maybe not a good husband those last couple of years, but a good father.'

'He'll have it to do all over again,' Pavlik said. 'Rachel Slattery and Emma Byrne are on their way back south with my deputies. Most likely Rachel will spend a good amount of time in prison.'

'The baby,' I said. 'It could be born in prison.' I wondered how that was going to go over with Mother Slattery. Happily, the baby had Ted to fight for him or her. And then there was Stephen. I had a hunch Rachel's brother would gladly take on their mother in order to protect his niece or nephew.

Ted stuck his head in. His swollen lips preceded him. 'Sorry to interrupt, but I wanted to let you know that Eric is riding back with me.'

'You're not going to take him back to school tonight, are you?'

Ted shook his head. 'No, he's going to stay with me in Brookhills and I'll drive him up on Sunday. It'll be good to have the company this weekend.'

'I know,' I said. 'I'll call you tomorrow.'

'Hey!' Yet another head around the corner. This one was Sarah's. 'Are you coming with me?'

I looked at Pavlik. 'We done?'

He sighed. 'Us? Not by a long shot, I fear. But yes, go home with Sarah for now. And I'll call *you* tomorrow, too.'

He stood up and gave me a quick kiss on the top of the head.

By the time we reached Brookhills, it was seven a.m. It had been my morning to open Uncommon Grounds, but I'd called Caron and explained, so she took my shift.

'I'm too wired to go home and sleep,' I said to Sarah as we came off the freeway ramp.

'Because you took down a couple of killers or because Pavlik said he was going to call you?'

'Both,' I admitted. 'Want to stop for coffee?'

'Sure.' Sarah turned on to Brookhill Road. 'I guess I won't be playing tennis today.'

'I'm sorry about Emma,' I said. 'I know she's your friend.'

'I liked her,' Sarah admitted. 'But did you see how she changed around Rachel? Emma is a strong woman, yet she let that little bitch lead her right into murder.'

'Rachel fooled a lot of people,' I said as we pulled into the parking lot. 'She was trying so hard to get away from her mother, that she *became* her mother.'

'There's probably something very Zen in that, but I'm too tired to think of it,' Sarah said, getting out of the car. 'Let's get that coffee.'

Sophie was up out of her chair the moment we entered. 'Is it true that frickin' Slattery girl is alive?'

'It is,' I said. 'And I'll tell you all about it when I get my coffee. Can I buy you a cup?'

'I already have some.' Sophie squinted at me. 'What are you up to?'

I was embarrassed. 'Nothing, I just . . . well, I know living in Brookhills is expensive.'

Sophie shrugged. 'It is, but I watch my pennies. I budget for coffee most days. I play tennis when it's nice so we can be outside and don't have to rent courts. I go on Red Hat outings that are inexpensive.' She patted my arm. 'You don't have to worry about me. I do damn fine for an old broad.'

Caron came out from behind the counter with three cups and a pot of coffee. She warmed up Sophie's coffee and then poured cups for herself, Sarah and me. 'OK, now give.'

I decided to summarize and then take questions. 'Rachel married Ted to get away from her family. Then she got pregnant. She and Emma Byrne were lovers and Rachel knew that if she had a baby, she would never be free of her mother.'

'Eve Whitaker is a controlling bitch,' Sophie said. 'Always was, always will be.'

'You know her?' I asked.

'Sure. We used to play tennis. She cheated.'

Caron looked puzzled. 'I don't get it. Ted was Rachel's . . . what do they call it? A beard?'

'Apparently so. Rachel didn't have the nerve to tell her mother she was gay.'

Sarah looked impatient. 'Listen, if Maggy tells this, it's going to take all day. Fact is, Rachel and Emma wanted to run away with the baby, but they knew both Ted and Rachel's mother would try to find them. So Rachel planted evidence to make it seem like Ted was cheating on her, then she planned to disappear. A convenient body turned up, but it wasn't dead so they killed it.'

I had nothing on Sarah, summarization-wise. She was a master.

'Oh!' I said, remembering. 'That guy who knocked me down when he came out of the dumpster. I bet that was Gretchen's boyfriend and he was looking for her.'

'Gretchen?' Caron asked.

'She was the woman I saw outside the dental clinic on Saturday. It was her body they used. According to Emma, Gretchen's boyfriend beat her up when he found out she was pregnant and probably tried to cause a miscarriage by kicking her in the stomach. It must have worked, because the autopsy showed Gretchen wasn't pregnant. I bet she took off right after that. She may even have been sleeping on that mattress out there.'

'Until she was killed on it,' Sarah muttered.

Caron put her hand over her mouth. 'That's why the sheriff's deputy was looking around back there this morning. I thought he was checking the lock.'

A rash of dumpster break-ins, no doubt.

'The mattress and the paint cans back there will be evidence,' I said. 'Plus the coat and the draperies that were dumped at the Hamilton.'

Seeing Sophie and Caron's puzzled faces, Sarah took up the story again. 'Rachel was supposed to meet Roger Karsten at the Hamilton, but she didn't go there. Instead she went to help Emma with the body. She knew, like everyone else in Brookhills, that Roger would only wait for a few minutes. By the time they got there with the body, he was long gone.'

'That's why Emma cancelled the tour that night.' I told Sarah. 'The one you were supposed to go on originally. They needed the place to themselves.'

I shook my head. 'You should have seen Emma's face when I told her Rachel's body had been found in Lake Michigan. She was absolutely shocked. I thought it was because she thought Ted might be involved.'

'Bet she sure as shit was trying to figure out how that body got from the hotel basement to the lake,' Sophie said.

A godawful sound erupted from beside me.

'Are you snoring?' I asked Sarah.

She sat up straight, startled. 'Of course not. Just resting my eyes.' She stood up and looked at me. 'I do need to get going, though. Need a lift home?'

We walked out to the Firebird. 'That was a short visit,' I said. 'Need your morning run?'

She snorted. 'You kidding? Ted and Emma were my running partners. Ted was suspected of killing his wife. Emma is going to be charged with Gretchen's murder. I'm lucky I got out unscathed. All that exercise is hazardous to your health.'

Twenty-One

'You know, truisms are really . . .' I searched for the word.

'True?' Pavlik guessed. It was Saturday again, a full week since Rachel's visit to me, and we were sitting on the couch in my living room. We were being careful with each other, but I thought we were both trying to act like we had before a week of hell had gotten between us.

'True. Yes.'

'Like what?' He pushed a lock of hair out of my eyes.

'Take your pick, but "the apple doesn't fall far from the tree" is the one I was thinking about. Rachel is her mother. She just doesn't know it.' I rubbed at my forehead.

'Headache?' Pavlik had me turn around and lie down face-up with my head in his lap. Then he started to massage my temples. 'Feel good?'

Good? To paraphrase Mae West, it was *so* good, it was bad. Very, very bad. I had a hunch it was 'bad' for Pavlik, too.

'Great,' I replied. The word came out a half octave higher than my usual pitch. I cleared my throat. 'I mean, it's wonderful. Don't stop.'

'OK.'

Judging by the hitch in his voice, he was finding the rubbing pretty pleasurable, as well. 'By the way,' Pavlik said, kneading his thumbs into the little notches by my shoulder blades, 'we've picked up Gretchen's boyfriend.'

'Are you going to charge him?'

'We'll try, but with just Emma's hearsay testimony of what Gretchen told her, it's going to be pretty hard to prove anything at this point.'

'It's so sad. The woman had nothing. It was like she was invisible.'

We were quiet for a few minutes.

'Have you seen Eric?'

'He and Ted came over for dinner last night.' I worked my shoulders a bit. Pavlik gave a little groan. 'I'm glad they've had some time to spend together. Ted's still pretty shook.'

'He's lucky you got there when you did.'

'You think they would have killed him?'

'Unless the hole she was digging in the back was for a pool. And they would have killed you, too.' Pavlik leaned down to kiss me on the lips.

I sighed, admittedly happy to be alive. 'Eric's pretty charged up about being a hero.'

'He's quite a kid.' Pavlik ran his hand down my bare arm. The weather had turned nice again and I was wearing a sleeveless shirt and shorts. The window next to us was open, a warm breeze lifting the curtains.

I knew the changeable Wisconsin spring was just waiting to betray us. My daffodils would stick their heads out one day and be buried by a blizzard the next. It was worth taking the risk, though, to enjoy the sunshine while it lasted. To trust, even if they got snowed occasionally.

No idiots, my daffodils.

I twisted around to kiss Pavlik.